Under His Protection: Brie's Submission #14

By
Red Phoenix

Heather,

I hope you enjoy Faelan's story. One of tragedy and empowerment.
Hugs! Red Phoenix

Under His Protection: Brie's Submission

Print Edition

RedPhoenix69@live.com

Edited by Jennifer Blackwell, Proofed by Becki Wyer and Marilyn Cooper
Cover by Viola Estrella
Formatted by BB eBooks
Phoenix symbol by Nicole Delfs

Adult Reading Material (18+)

Dedication

My dear fans, what an incredible journey this book has been! I have long known Faelan's story but it has been locked inside my head waiting for the right moment to be unleashed.

That moment is now.

Let me just say that as I wrote the last words all I could think was, "OMG OMG OMG!"

I would like to thank all the muses who made this story before you possible.

Faelan - Todd Wallace (Blue Eyes)

Brie Bennett

Sir Thane Davis

Tono Nosaka

Rytsar Durov

Master Anderson

Marquis Gray

Mary Wilson

Lea Taylor

Ms. Clark

Master Coan

Mr. & Mrs. Reynolds

Baron

Captain

Candy

Boa

Kylie

Lisa Wallace

Mr. and Mrs. Wallace

and even

Greg Holloway

I have been writing this series since 2012

If you have followed the Brie series then you know things that were mentioned in the very first novellas have an important place now as the puzzle comes together for Faelan's story.

It's exhilarating to see it unfold!

I hope you enjoy reading Faelan's journey as much as I have adored writing it.

The truth about his past has been a long time in coming - 5 years to be exact

As always, I would like to thank

MrRed, my Sir and biggest supporter

But I would also like to thank:

Brandi, a longtime fan, cheerleader and graphic genius

Becki, another longtime fan, encourager and proofer extraordinaire

Marilyn, super fan of Brie and Sir, travel buddy and true craft artisan

Steve, fan of Brie, skilled home chef and gracious host

Brenda, longtime fan, creative soul, and my go-to gal

Autumn, an amazing blogger and longtime Brie fan

Nicole, dedicated fan and designer of my beloved Phoenix

Julia, a longtime fan of Red herself, and creator of many laughs

Little Phoenix, humorous mini-me with a creative soul and the heart to help

MrRedJr, humble genius who introduced me to dubstep and still works behind the scenes

LemonLark, a girl after my own heart and the artist behind my avatar for the vids

Paul, formatter supreme, forward thinker – consistently perfect and dedicated to authors

Anthony, right-hand man, can't thank him enough for the time investment, advice, and his belief in the future of the Brie series

To every fan of Brie – new and old. Your excitement for Brie's story, your love of the characters, your heartfelt messages and your generosity toward me has changed my life.

I was a writer from the moment I could scribble a word, but I didn't become an author until I connected with readers like you.

Contents

It Begins…

People were going to pay—a lot of people.

Did they really think he could stand being humiliated and beaten without doing something drastic and permanent?

A man can only be pushed so far…

By the time he was finished, they would all be lying dead in their own blood.

Justice would be served.

He reached out and caressed the AK-12 lying on the passenger seat and glanced back at the satchel of grenades. Only a few more guns were needed before he could launch his attack. It was going to be a bloodbath.

This was war.

Faelan watched the video Mary was streaming live from her phone in Italy. He smiled when he saw Marquis guiding Brie across the dance floor in the center of the courtyard, surrounded by their large, enthusiastic circle of family—some by blood and others bonded through the BDSM community.

Both Brie and Marquis were important to him.

Blossom had saved Faelan's life without knowing it the first day they met, and Marquis had saved his sanity when Faelan lost her.

Mary turned the phone back around and smiled. "You can see Brie's having a good time. Married twit that she is." Her amused laughter made him grin. "So let's see how Sir Davis is handling his new *collar*."

Turning the camera around, Mary scanned the crowd until she found the man. Davis was speaking to Nosaka. It looked like a serious conversation, and Faelan took note that both were looking in Brie's direction as they spoke to one another.

He still felt a twinge of pain remembering that night of the Collaring Ceremony when Brie stood before him to present her collar. He closed his eyes as that excruciating moment played out in his mind…

Come to me, blossom…

Standing a little taller, Faelan felt a deep sense of pride knowing that he would be collaring Brie in front of everyone in attendance at the Submissive Training Center.

He'd envisioned this moment ever since he'd discovered she was a submissive at the beach house. It was the driving force that kept him striving forward during his darkest hours.

Brie was meant for him.

He'd understood that truth the moment he'd caught her in his arms outside the school, saving her from a violent encounter with the pavement. One look into those honey-colored eyes…and his life had meaning.

The guilt he'd carried all those years as a survivor suddenly lifted when he saw that breathtaking smile.

She was the reason he'd been spared.

She was the reason he'd enrolled in the Dominant Training Course to become the man worthy of her.

She was the reason Thane Davis had mentored him personally, grooming him to claim Brie as his own.

After all those years living in pain, the Universe suddenly made sense—it no longer seemed cruel and indifferent.

Faelan had worked hard, taking on both his business classes and his nightly Dominant training without complaint. He would do anything to be the Dominant worthy of her.

As Brie approached Faelan with her collar, he smiled back at her with confidence. All the pain of the past and the sacrifices he'd made disappeared when he looked in those eyes.

Mine…

He furrowed his brow when she suddenly stopped with a look of uncertainty on her face.

Come, blossom, he commanded silently when she gazed into his eyes.

But Brie turned and he suddenly felt the first hint of

panic.

Don't…

His whole body went numb as he watched his blossom walk toward Thane Davis and bow low at his feet.

Faelan shook his head, not able to accept what was happening.

Brie was *his*.

Relief flooded through him when Davis rejected her offer. It was confirmation that even the Headmaster knew she was meant for him.

Although Faelan realized she had been humiliated by the man's public refusal, he would be the one to ease her pain and mend her broken heart.

All that mattered was Brie.

Faelan was set to follow her out of the Training Center when the Headmaster called out to her as she walked away.

"Brie… Come back and face me."

Faelan's mouth went dry as he watched Brie approach Davis a second time and kneel before the Headmaster.

Closing his eyes in pain when the chime sounded, beginning the formal Collaring Ceremony, Faelan endured. It took all his strength to remain silent even though every bone in his body longed to stop the travesty that was happening.

Feeling a hand on his shoulder, Faelan opened his eyes to find Tono looking at him with compassion. He jerked away, not needing sympathy from his rival.

Mary's gaze was equally sympathetic, which infuriated Faelan even more. He didn't want anyone's pity.

This is what I deserve, he thought with resolution as he continued to watch. *Why should I experience happiness when the boy I killed lies dead in the ground?*

Turning his focus back on Brie, Faelan forced himself to remain still as she spoke the vows that were meant for him. His lips twitched as he watched Davis pick Brie up and carry her to his office—adding insult to injury.

Nosaka left soon after, keeping to himself as he made his way to the elevator.

Coward…

Faelan glanced at Mary and snarled under his breath. "This is bullshit."

"Do you want to leave?"

"No," he scoffed. "I'm playing this out to the bitter end."

She frowned a little, but stayed beside him while everyone else kept their distance and avoided eye contact.

He hated this. Hated knowing what Brie was doing with Davis while he stood here trying not to look as devastated as he felt.

But he had to stay—for her sake.

Faelan had to see Brie's face when they returned. He *needed* to see that she was truly happy with her choice. If there was any indication that she wasn't, he would snatch her out of Davis's arms no matter the cost to himself.

So he endured the minutes ticking by as he stared down the hallway, waiting for Brie's return. The whole time suffering the humiliation of whispers around him—for her.

Finally, Davis returned with Brie walking proudly beside him. She was naked from the waist up with the word "Mine" written across her chest.

It was as if the Universe was pointedly laughing at him.

Faelan remained resolute, seeking Brie's gaze. When their eyes finally connected, his heart skipped a beat. There was no look of regret, only an inner light that blinded him with its joy.

All was lost.

He cleared his throat and growled angrily at Mary, "I'm outta here."

"Do you want me to go with you?"

"What, and miss all the excitement?"

When she persisted, he chose a more blunt answer, needing to get far away from this place and everything associated with Brie.

"Look, I'd rather be alone."

Faelan made a quick exit, avoiding Brie, unable to deal with the alternate reality she'd just created.

As he drove toward his empty apartment, he released his mounting emotions by revving up the old Mustang and letting her fly down the highway.

For a brief moment the terrified expression of Trevor's face just before impact filled his vision. Faelan immediately slammed on his brakes and pulled to the side of the road, breathing heavily.

He hadn't experienced those visions since…he'd met Brie.

Why am I here? he wondered. He continued his drive home, but the more he thought about it, the more agitated he became until he finally screamed, "Why the fuck am I here?!"

The silence of the dead greeted his question.

With resignation, he pulled up to his apartment and shut off the car. He stared at his place as the walls of his personal hell closed in around him.

There was no escape from this. He was foolish to have thought there was.

Walking into the apartment, Faelan sighed as he turned off the chocolate fountain he'd made ready for Brie. He put away all the tools he'd laid out, and turned off the music. Heading to the kitchen to grab a bottle of tequila, he unscrewed the cap and tossed it on the counter. He walked to the couch and switched on the TV, needing to distract himself from everything.

Instead of helping, it only made him more agitated. Faelan got up and began pacing, gulping down the liquor.

His blossom was with another man. Oh God, how that hurt…

Not mine, he thought with disbelief.

Tipping the bottle up, he began chugging. The warmth of the tequila started to have its desired effect and he was able to sit back down.

"Okay, okay…" he told himself. "You fucked up and lost her. Your one chance, and now she's gone…"

Those last words cut like a knife and he howled in pain.

The rest of the evening became a blur as the tequila settled in and had its way with him. He woke up the next morning on the floor, clutching the empty bottle.

When he sat up, his head began pounding but he violently resisted the urge to puke on the black marble.

His bender had only succeeded in getting him through one night, leaving him weak and in greater pain the next day. How the hell was he supposed to survive the rest of his life without her?

Faelan stumbled to the bathroom and puked his guts out. Afterward, he splashed his face with cold water and gazed into the mirror. The whites of his eyes were red from drinking too much, and he had the look of a haunted man.

He knew that look well.

"You have to get her back," he told his reflection. "You're never going to survive without her."

Faelan's heart began racing as he was renewed with hope. Last night he'd convinced himself it was over, but it didn't have to be. Brie didn't know who he was because he'd never let her in.

That's why she made the wrong decision. If she knew, she would never have walked away.

Even though he understood it was a long shot, Faelan talked himself into intervening. The girl had only been collared one night. There was still time to get her back.

There had to be.

Faelan immediately called in sick and spent the day recovering from his bender. He needed to be fully aware and on point when he spoke with Brie again. It was time to open himself up and let her in.

He tried to ignore the rage he felt against Davis. The man could have any sub he wanted; there was no reason to take blossom when the Headmaster had specifically trained him up to claim her.

It was a slap in the face.

But Faelan would not back down. He was willing to fight Davis head-on if he had to. He'd do anything to get Brie back. Grabbing his keys, he drove to the tobacco shop, hoping to catch her after her shift ended. When he didn't see her car there, he ventured inside.

There was a slobbishly dressed kid at the counter, busy playing some game on his phone. Faelan smiled to himself, knowing getting information out of the boy would be easy. "Hey, man, do you know where Brie is today? The chick owes me some money."

"She didn't show up, so I'm here on my day off," he grumbled.

"Do you know if she will be in tomorrow?"

"No, the bitch ain't coming back 'til Monday."

Faelan didn't appreciate the turd's disrespectful reference to Brie, but let it slide. "You know what hours she'll be working? I don't want her to slip out before I get my cash."

"What's in it for me, dickhead?"

Faelan slipped a twenty onto the counter. "I get it. Your time is worth something."

The boy grabbed the cash and huffed in irritation as he got out the schedule and looked it up. "She's working the day shift and gets off at five."

"That's all I needed to know. Thanks."

"Whatever…" the asshole answered, looking disinterested as he stared at his phone, resuming his game.

Faelan left the shop feeling unsettled, knowing he would have to wait several more days—each day would bind Brie to Davis more, but there was nothing Faelan could do other than wait and be patient.

If they were meant to be, nothing could prevent it.

He held on to that hope.

Faelan received a lot of grief when he called work on Monday telling them a second time that he wasn't coming in. With a store inspection looming, his boss was severely displeased.

It didn't matter. He was willing to lose his job for Brie. A job could be replaced, but Brie? She was everything.

Faelan waited for her, leaning against his Mustang casually, trying to hide the fact he was nervous. He couldn't afford to fuck this up.

When Brie finally came out of the shop, all his fears disappeared. Her aura calmed his soul and reminded him why he had been so affected by her the moment they'd met.

Brie hadn't noticed him standing there in her hurry to get to her car.

Faelan called out as he walked up. "Brie! Brie Bennett."

She turned, looking surprised to see him. "What are you doing here?"

"I've been waiting to talk with you alone."

"I can't," she exclaimed nervously. "I don't think Sir would approve."

Faelan kept his eye on the prize and said calmly, "But this is between us—it doesn't involve him."

She looked as if she was about to flee, so he gently took hold of her arm. "We're just going to talk. What's the harm in that?"

"I don't think we should."

"Brie," he replied, smiling sadly. "Don't you think I deserve an explanation?"

"Todd…" She quickly corrected herself, addressing him properly. "Mr. Wallace."

He didn't care for being called by his surname—it created a distance between them he didn't want—but he forced himself to shrug it off.

"We're two of a kind, you and me."

Faelan was encouraged when he drew near to her and she didn't move. "I knew the minute I met you that you and I were meant to be. Hell, my one thought this whole time has been to become the man, the Dom, you need."

She replied angrily, "It didn't appear that way at my graduation."

"Blossom." He smiled, saying her pet name with tenderness. "You should know that I didn't touch Mary."

Shaking her head, Brie turned toward her car. "I heard Mary… Don't even go there."

He moved toward her with caution, afraid she might bolt. "Look, Mary needed a little pain so I delivered what she asked for. There was no intercourse involved."

Brie glared at him as if he was lying. "If that was the case, you should have explained that to me when I asked, but you didn't! And now…it doesn't matter." She put her hands on her hips. "I'm Sir's now. There is no going back."

Her words were like daggers to his heart but still he persisted, needing her to understand. "We are meant to be together, Brie." He backed her up against the car, putting an arm on either side of her. "Headmaster Davis stole you from me. Why the hell did he spend all that extra time training me to be your Dominant just to steal you away?"

He could tell she was swayed by his presence—their natural chemistry affecting her as much as it did him. But the blood in his veins ran cold when she looked up and said, "I chose him."

"It's because of that damn Mary, isn't it?" he demanded. "She's the one who screwed it up for us."

"When I asked if you wanted Mary, you answered, 'Yes.' I knew then you didn't care about me."

"What? Did you expect me to lie to you? Any guy who told you he wasn't attracted to the girl would not have been telling the truth. Come on, Brie…" He lifted her chin, forcing her to look him in the eye. "Just because I find her attractive doesn't mean I want to collar her. I was clear about that."

Brie glanced away, his candid answer having a clear effect on her. She scooted away from him and headed to the driver's side of her car.

Faelan let her go, stating quietly, "I deserve a chance."

Her hands were trembling as she fumbled with her key, trying to unlock the car. "It's too late."

He had to convince her that it wasn't.

"I need you, blossom." Faelan returned to her, covering her trembling hand with his. "*You* are my reason."

Brie slowly pulled the key back out of the lock and looked up at him. "No…don't say that."

"Brie, I didn't understand who I was until I met you.

You opened my eyes to the truth and freed me from the hell I've been suffering." He saw the tears in her eyes, and knew he had her full attention. "Don't turn your back on me now."

She shook her head. "Please…stop."

"If you knew the truth, you would not be so callous toward me."

"I'm not being callous, Todd." He smiled to himself, gratified she'd called him by his first name. "But this," she gestured at the two of them, "doesn't do either of us any good. We can't change what happened graduation night. I—"

It was time. Time to share his past with her. It was a natural response to lift his hand and caress her cheek. He leaned closer, ready to speak the words he'd held back for so long.

"Brie, is this man harassing you? Do you want me to call the police?" Mr. Reynolds called from the shop's doorway.

The connection was instantly broken—his chance evaporating before his eyes as Brie backed away.

"No, everything is fine, Mr. Reynolds," she answered. "We're done here. I was just leaving."

She unlocked her car door and glanced at Faelan. "Don't talk to me again. You'll only get yourself in trouble." Jumping into her vehicle, Brie took off without looking back.

How could it just end like that?

Faelan glanced at Mr. Reynolds. The man would never know the injustice he'd dished out by interfering.

Getting into his blue Mustang, Faelan took a few

minutes to collect himself before heading out. Rather than driving back home, he drove straight to work. There was no need to indulge in another bender. He'd just have to remain patient and trust there would come a day when he would get his blossom back.

Faelan shook his head as the memory faded. He couldn't have been more wrong about Brie, but he didn't regret what happened because it eventually led him to the woman he truly loved—the surly sub who'd prevented him from collaring Brie in the first place.

Mary turned the camera back on herself. "So yeah, there are a lot of people here at the wedding, and you'd think Brie would be eating up all the attention but the girl is totally fixated on Sir Davis. Like a lovesick cow or something."

"You jealous?" he asked with a grin.

Mary burst out laughing. "No way. A ring around my finger *and* a collar? I think I would suffocate and die."

He chuckled, not taking offense at her declaration. Mary was a free spirit. He'd always known that about her. But she had something that Brie lacked—a black hole in her heart. It was something he could relate to.

Mary's cavernous need turned most people away, but Faelan understood the gravity and weight of it. Because he understood it, he could appreciate how far she'd come. It was his mission to help Mary not only overcome her past, but truly be set free from it.

Despite being one of the top graduates from the Submissive Training Center, the horrors of her childhood still held a tight grip on her soul.

Becoming a student at The Center had been the best thing to happen to her, not only because of the excellent instruction she'd received, but also because it gave Mary a sense of belonging. In a world of trolls and ingenuous people, the staff and pupils at The Center had provided her with real human connection.

As much as Mary clawed and scratched at those closest to her, Faelan knew she'd be lost without them—especially Brie. Mary would rather die than admit she not only cared about Brie but admired her.

No other female in her life had stuck by Mary's side through good times and bad like Brie had, including Mary's own mother.

It was the reason Faelan had insisted she go to Brie's wedding, despite the fact he had to stay behind in Colorado. The look of excitement when Mary opened the invitation and saw she'd been asked to act as one of Brie's bridesmaids had been deeply gratifying to him.

"Can you believe Sir Thane Davis invited *me* to be a bridesmaid?" Mary smiled to herself, mumbling as she stared at the invitation, "What the hell was he thinking?"

"Of course he asked you. Davis knows you're important to Brie."

She looked up at him with tears in her eyes. That

brief moment of vulnerability was a cherished gift. Each chink in her heavy armor, a victory.

Mary chuckled to herself as if he'd made a joke. "I can't. I don't know why he even asked knowing the situation."

"What do you mean?"

"You're not able to travel yet." She gave him a bemused smile as she stroked her new collar. "You're my Master now. It's my duty to take care of you…" With a seductive grin, she reached down to graze her fingernails against his crotch.

"True. You are *mine* now and your greatest duty is to obey me."

"I know…" She got that naughty twinkle in her eye as she started to kneel between his legs.

Whenever confronted with genuine feelings, Mary tended to resort to sex or baring her claws. It was her standard mode of operation, but Faelan wanted to stop those old habits and replace them with something new. It required patience on his part and thoughtful guidance, because he must to be careful not to step on her fragile ego.

Grabbing her by both hands, Faelan helped her stand on her feet. "As your Master, I can use you any way I desire, correct?"

"Pretty much," she answered, staring at him lustfully. "And for me the rougher the better."

"Then you, my slave, will buy plane tickets so you can attend the wedding."

Releasing his hold on her, Faelan stood back and watched for her reaction. It was a test of sorts.

"A good slave would *not* leave her Master," she insisted.

"A good slave would obey her Master," he corrected, leaning forward to kiss her on the lips.

"But I can't leave you," she stated earnestly.

Faelan suspected she was harboring fears about his health, so he assured her, "I will be fine. I'm certain my mother will be thrilled to baby me while you're gone." He put his hands on her shoulders and said, "My desire is to see you standing in line at your best friend's wedding."

"Brie's not my best friend!" Mary protested.

He raised his eyebrow. "Seriously?"

"Don't you *ever* tell her that, don't even hint about it. God knows I would never hear the end of it if you do."

It was like watching a teenager vehemently deny a high school crush. He cupped her chin and told her, "I got your back, woman. Your secret's safe with me."

Mary smiled begrudgingly, shaking her head as she stared at the invitation again. "Heh, I'm going to be a part of Brie's wedding…"

Faelan was grateful to Davis. Whether the man knew it or not, he had cemented her relationship with Brie. Now Brie would remain forever a part of Mary's life, a part of her sisterhood of sorts.

Mary needed that stability in her life.

"You know, I never thought I could ever feel excited about going to a wedding. But dang, I could just squeeze Brie 'til her eyes pop out."

"Best to wait until after the wedding to squeeze her, then."

Mary laughed, wrapping her arms around his waist and looking up at him with a childlike grin. "Thank you, Master."

His heart skipped a beat. When Mary looked at him that way, it stirred his protective instincts. Despite every emotionally charged roadblock Mary had thrown his way, Faelan had faithfully navigated them because he knew how much she needed him.

The abuse at the hands of her own father had warped her sense of worth. To hide her self-contempt from the world, Mary had harnessed her beauty and used it as a weapon.

Teasing men with her feminine wiles, but never letting them get close, was a game to her. Any person, man or woman, who dared to penetrate her inner circle was destined to be crushed and destroyed.

He knew that was *her* truth.

But no matter how many times he'd endured her well-aimed barbs, Faelan held on to the *real* truth. Mary was a fighter. The woman within, the resilient soul who longed to be freed from the chains of her past, had an inner strength and beauty few possessed.

The abandonment by her mother and the cruelty of her father had defined her before. By accepting his collar, she'd broken the first chain.

Today was the second. She'd allowed Brie into her inner circle, even admitted it in a roundabout way to him.

"I'll miss you…Master," she confessed, looking at him demurely.

Faelan felt a stirring in his spirit every time she addressed him as Master. Although he loathed the idea of being without her for an entire week, forced to endure his mother's constant doting, it would be worth it for Mary's sake. He felt certain both girls would benefit from the deeper connection this wedding celebration would bring.

So while Mary set about getting ready for the big trip, Faelan busied himself arranging a special gift for her while they were apart. His intent was to take this simple wedding obligation and make it the next step in Mary's metamorphosis.

Transformation

After showing him the reception festivities, Mary turned the phone camera back on herself. "So, Master, you mentioned earlier that you have a task for me tonight. Will you tell me what it is now?" she asked, while the celebration continued behind her.

"Naturally," he answered with a wicked grin. "I want you to go to bed alone. Put on the clothing I sent with you." He could only imagine the look on her face when she unwrapped the box.

"There is also a piece of cloth to use as a blindfold."

"Ooh…I'm liking the sound of this."

He chuckled lustfully.

In the spirit of the celebration, he thought it would be amusing if Mary wore virginal white high heels and nothing else.

"You will text me before you lie on the bed and wait. Someone will be joining you to observe you while you fulfill the task."

"What's my task?"

"He will observe you masturbating."

"Go on…" Mary begged, clearly excited.

"You must come as many times as he requests without fail. If you prove worthy, he will take a picture of your wet pussy and send it to me so I know you've completed the first task."

"I love the way you think," she complimented, raising an eyebrow. "You're just so dirty…"

"And you are the girl to fulfill my filthiest desires."

"That I am, Master." Caressing her collar with her fingertips, she laughed again. Faelan was captivated by the smile on her face. When Mary's defenses were down, she was truly the most beautiful girl he'd ever seen. "It's not the same without you here, Faelan."

"Well, I am about to change that," he told her with a smirk, knowing how excited she would be after hearing his plans. "If your observer is pleased by your performance tonight, he has permission to use your body as a canvas for his art."

Mary's eyes grew wide as she asked breathlessly, "What kind of art?"

"I know how you love needle play."

"Oh, you are too good to me!"

"That's not the best part," Faelan added. "The man who is joining you is the one and only Master O himself."

Mary's jaw dropped when she heard the name. Faelan had never forgotten that night at the Haven when Master O had requested Mary join him and she had turned down the world-renowned Dom to scene with Faelan instead.

Her sacrifice that night deserved to be rewarded, and

it brought Faelan immense joy to give her this gift now.

"Faelan, I don't even know what to say…" Mary murmured, tears welling up in her eyes.

He hadn't expected such an emotional response and was touched by it. "I told you I would give you the world when I collared you."

She shook her head with a flirtatious grin. "You're too good to me."

Faelan had saved the best for last and proudly announced, "I have instructed Master O to create an intricate and original design. You will be enjoying his unique attention for hours."

"Oh my god," she cried in excitement.

"When he's finished, he plans to take a picture of you for his gallery."

"I'm going to be on his wall?" she asked, flashing that beautiful smile Faelan coveted.

"As you should be," he answered proudly.

Mary's excited expression suddenly changed to concern. "It doesn't seem fair. You alone over there, while I'm having all the fun."

"Trust me, your full participation is all I need from you tonight."

"Well, if you insist." She smiled flirtatiously, batting her eyes at the camera. "Of course, I will have to find a way to pay you back."

"I look forward to it."

Faelan waited until he received her text. He sat down on the couch and slowly unbuttoned his jeans. Freeing his cock from his boxers, he began to slowly stroke it, imagining Mary lying on the bed, blindfolded in her white heels as she waited for the night's events to begin.

What he hadn't told Mary was that he had asked Master O to call him and set the phone on the nightstand so Faelan could listen to their exchange.

He heard the slight tremble in Mary's voice when she answered the venerated Master just before she began her first task. He listened to the moans and cries of passion that followed as she played with herself for Master O's pleasure, coming again and again as he requested.

After the fourth orgasm, Master O announced her task was complete and sent a picture from Mary's phone to Faelan of her blonde pussy all pink, wet, and swollen.

The real fun began for Mary as Master O laid out his tools and explained to her what he was going to do. "I will be ornamenting your back tonight, but before I begin I want to slide a needle through each nipple and play with them as you kiss me."

"You're going to pierce them?"

"Temporarily," he answered. "First, I squeeze your areola like this."

Mary moaned passionately in response to his touch.

"You will breathe in deeply and hold it. When I command, you will breathe out slowly as I push the needle into your nipple." He added with a low seductive laugh, "Enjoy the pain."

As he picked up one of the needles, he told her, "I want you to hold this needle for a moment. Imagine how it will feel as it pierces your skin."

"It's so long," she commented breathlessly.

"It is," he agreed. "Now breathe in…"

Faelan stroked himself while waiting for Master O to

command she breathe out. When the order came, Faelan heard Mary's gasp of pain as the needle penetrated her nipple.

"And now for the other." The man growled huskily. "Breathe in and hold." He paused for several moments, drawing out the anticipation before commanding, "And breathe out…"

Mary gasped again and then moaned afterward.

"And now my kiss…" he ordered in a deep voice.

Master O took a picture afterward of Mary lying on the bed looking sexy in her blindfold, each of her nipples pierced by long silver needles. Her relaxed smile spoke to the pleasure she'd enjoyed in the exchange.

Faelan orgasmed several times that evening to the sound of Mary's cries of pleasure and pain, catching the euphoria in her voice when she began to fly from the subhigh inspired by Master O's unique art.

It was a long and very satisfying session for them all.

In Faelan's mind, Master O was simply an instrument. An instrument he'd employed for the pleasure and vindication for his submissive. He felt no jealousy toward the man, toward any of them he invited to play with her.

They were simply a means to an end.

By accepting his collar, Mary had finally made an outward commitment to him. He would honor that commitment by slowly unraveling the thorny vines that still bound her heart.

There would come a day when she would break free. She was destined for more. He would see that she achieved it, that was his goal and his relentless pursuit.

In the meantime, he would bide his time exploring the limitless depths of BDSM with her—the two of them having a passion for kinky and challenging experiences. When she finally reached the other side, it would be a glorious victory for her and absolution for him and his past.

Faelan had trouble going to sleep after such a stimulating session, leaving him ample time to lie in the dark and reminisce about the changes that had come over Mary since the day she'd knelt at his feet in the hospital and offered him her total submission.

He hadn't dared to believe it was real until the moment he'd wrapped his belt around her neck as a makeshift collar and pulled her up to kiss those sexy lips, claiming Mary as his.

Since then, he'd seen significant changes come over her. Knowing Mary's harsh exterior, he was pleased to discover she had the gentle heart of a caregiver. In his weakest moment, as he struggled to recover from the transplant, she became his strength, coaxing him back to health with her tender but demanding hands.

No task was beneath her as she made sure every instruction from his physician was followed to the T. Being a pharmacist by trade, she held the doctor's instructions in the highest regard and worked tirelessly to make Faelan whole again.

It was humbling to see a woman so proud and closed

off from the world become an angel of mercy at his lowest points. She was proof that their dark pasts did not have to define their futures, now that they had one another to rely on.

It gutted him whenever he thought of Mary's father hurting her. What would she have been like if she'd grown up in a normal household raised by two loving parents?

The truth—he'd probably never have met her had that been the case. Mary would have already graduated from college with a doting husband by her side, and started on her family of 2.5 kids.

Mary needed him. That was the only reason Faelan had earned her collar and devotion.

But if there had ever been any doubt about her feelings toward him, they'd been erased during his recovery. In his hour of need, she'd come to him and accepted his collar, albeit reluctantly.

Giving Faelan that level of commitment seemed to have opened Mary up, allowing her to embrace another side of herself that he'd always suspected was there.

Still unable to sleep, Faelan turned to lie on his back and started stroking his cock again as he thought back on one particularly erotic bandaging session. It was the night he gave Mary her sub name.

"Faelan, don't you move a damn muscle. I've got soup on the stove and bread in the oven. Now let me help with those bandages before you reinjure yourself."

"There's no need to fuss over me," he growled, tired of being in pain and being helpless like a baby in front of his newly claimed submissive.

"Look, I'm only following your doctor's orders," she stated. "Don't even *think* of trying to help. Lie there and be a good boy."

He grabbed her wrist and pulled her to him, ignoring the pain. "I'm not a boy, Mary, and you can't expect me to lie here passively when you bend over like that." He glanced at her tantalizing cleavage.

"I want you to play with my girls, Faelan," she answered, pulling away. "But only after I redress your wounds and you eat."

"What if I say no?"

Mary smiled mischievously. "Then I'll get some rope and tie you down until I'm finished. Either way, these bandages are getting redressed."

Faelan conceded, but he noticed the seductive way Mary went about her business: bending down at an angle that gave him the best view of her breasts, and lightly brushing his skin with an erect nipple as she meticulously followed the procedure of cleaning and dressing his wound.

After she was finished, Mary bent down dangerously close to his lips and whispered alluringly, "And now I must get your lunch."

Before he could grab her, she was out the door laughing in wicked delight.

Faelan shook his head in frustration and amusement. Ever since collaring her, he'd felt like a new man. A man with purpose and a good woman to love.

Thank God, Ren Nosaka had agreed to the transplant even though Faelan had resented the offer in the beginning. He'd been ready to die when the Asian Dom arrived. Truly, if it hadn't been for Nosaka's persistence, he wouldn't have agreed to the surgery and would be dead right now.

That was a sobering thought…

It was a stroke of pure genius when Brie suggested Mary take her place when she suddenly had to leave for China.

Faelan had given up on ever seeing Mary again. When she walked through that hospital door, he was unprepared. The look of shock and betrayal on her face when she saw his condition hurt him deeply.

It wasn't until that moment he realized what a coward he'd been. Whining about the insidious itching and crippling pain when he should have been concentrating on one thing—healing.

When she ran from him, Faelan had a moment of clarity.

He immediately called his mother and asked her to bring his best suit. He'd let the girl push him away before, and he wasn't about to let that happen again. A collar around her neck would take the pressure off them both.

Not having to worry about how tomorrow would affect their lives allowed them the time and freedom to find their way together.

He understood the level of commitment he was asking from her. He'd avoided it before, responding to her restless nature. But they both needed stability.

With her willing submission came a transformation in Mary. A calmness and assuredness he hadn't seen before. It was reflected in simple things like the way she relaxed against him when he held her and her soft, even breathing at night—now that her night terrors were a thing of the past.

For the first time, he felt the allure of a real future together.

Mary came back with a tray of food. What he noticed first as she walked into the room was her unbuttoned blouse, exposing those lovely breasts she'd been teasing him with.

"I hope you're hungry," she said as she walked over to him, swaying her hips seductively.

Faelan reach out his hand and caressed the swell of her breast. "I'm definitely hungry for these."

"And they're all yours as soon as you eat everything here."

He glanced at the tray, surprised by the amount of food she'd prepared. Not only was there a huge bowl of soup, but a hunk of bread and a dish of spaghetti squash. "I'm not even hungry. No way I can eat all that."

Mary wiggled her breasts in front of him. "Are you sure you aren't hungry?"

He lunged forward to kiss one and groaned in pain from the effort, falling back against the headboard. "Oh God, that hurts…"

Mary set the tray down and rushed to him. "I'm sorry, baby. I didn't mean for you to hurt yourself."

Although he was suffering real pain, the moment her

breasts were close enough, he grabbed her around the waist and brought that sweet nipple to his mouth. Mary struggled unconvincingly as he sucked and nibbled on her delicious flesh, momentarily forgetting his pain as his cock stiffened between his legs.

"Oh, I see how it is…taking advantage of your nurse. I could have your head for this."

Faelan unzipped his pants and exposed his rigid shaft. "Are you speaking about this head, per chance?"

"You're so bad," she teased.

"Why don't you lick it and tell me how *bad* it is."

Mary smiled up at him as Faelan pushed her head toward his crotch, groaning in satisfaction when her lips made contact.

"You're pretty tangy, mister."

"Suck on it, nurse. I'm sure if you swallow it whole it'll go down smoothly."

Faelan felt a stabbing pain in his side, but he ignored it, enjoying watching his cock disappear down her throat far too much. No one could deepthroat a man like Mary. She was in a class all by herself.

He leaned his head back, using the pain as a vehicle to propel the intensity of his orgasm. Chills covered his skin as he felt his mounting release build.

"Oh God, don't stop," he commanded as he came, grabbing the back of her head and pumping his seed deep in her throat. Mary never gagged, taking his thrusts with gusto.

White-hot pain shot through his body at the end of his climax, taking his breath away. It added to the intensity of the experience and he cried out in animalistic passion after it passed.

"Was it satisfying?" she asked, gently licking his cock as she looked at him with those lustful eyes that stirred his soul.

He petted her hair. "You are a slice of heaven in a crazy world."

Swirling her tongue around the head of his cock, she smiled. "Can't say I've ever been called that before."

"Well, you are, my sexy angel."

Mary laughed. "I think you must be feverish. This girl ain't no angel, baby."

He pulled her up and held her close. "You are *my* angel. You've given me a whole new life." A name came to mind and he shared it with her. "I've wondered what your sub name would be because nothing seemed to fit. I know what it is now."

She pulled away to look at him. "I've been curious myself. Have to admit I was getting slightly concerned since you haven't given me one yet. But then, I'd rather not have one than be forced to answer to some ridiculous nickname."

"It's Celtic in origin, like mine. You pronounce it Awn-ya although it's spelled quite differently. Any guesses to the meaning?"

Mary shook her head. "Not making a fool of myself by guessing, but I do like the sound of it."

"The name means radiance."

"Radiance?" she questioned with a laughing snort.

He took her face in his hands and told her solemnly, "You guided me out of the darkness. You, Mary Wilson, are my angel of light."

She looked at him strangely, saying nothing. He was unsure if she was considering a polite way to tell him the name sucked, but as her eyes pooled with tears, he realized he'd hit the mark with the name.

He smiled at her. "There's no reason to cry."

"You don't understand," Mary said, swiping at her tears. "I've been called a whore all my life. I came to believe it and even embraced the title. But you…you're changing me."

"No. I'm only exposing what's already there."

"It scares me," she confessed.

"Why?"

"I don't know."

He wrapped his arms around her. "There's no reason to be scared, *awnya.* I love you and would never hurt you."

She settled against him but was tense in his arms. However, as the minutes passed she eventually relaxed in his embrace. "*Awnya*, huh? I could get used to that…"

He brushed her blonde hair back to gaze at her, his heart overflowing with love. Mary seemed to grow uncomfortable under his intense gaze, however, and pulled away.

Taking on the role as his nurse, she announced, "So now that you've got your fun, my naughty patient, it's time for you to eat!"

Mary remained a complicated woman, but it made him love her all the more.

Mystery Package

Mary had just returned from Italy the day before, and was heading out the front door determined to restock their dwindling grocery supply when he heard her cry out in surprise.

"What's wrong?"

She came back inside with a stunned look on her face, holding up a DVD to him. "Did you do this?"

Faelan felt the hairs rise on the back of his neck. "That didn't come from me."

The smile on Mary's face disappeared as she stared at the DVD case. "If it wasn't you, then…?"

"It must have been your mysterious benefactor," Faelan finished. He was unnerved that the man had returned to Mary's life—and he was certain it was a dude, although the person's identity had never been discovered. Even more unsettling was knowing the man had tracked Mary down to this place.

Faelan remembered the day when Mary had shared a sweet childhood memory of an anonymous donor leaving gifts on her doorstep. Faelan thought it was endearing at the time. However, it took on a whole different tone now that she was an adult.

"Did the person leave you any clues?"

"No, like before it's just the DVD. But it's the latest Disney movie, *Beauty and the Beast,* and it doesn't come out in theaters for two more weeks!" Mary squealed in delight.

"Don't you find it a little odd that your benefactor started up again after all these years?"

"Hey, I'm not about to look a gift horse in the mouth, buddy." She danced around in a circle as if the movie was her partner. "It's not every day you get your hands on the newest movie before it's released in theaters."

Faelan could see how happy Mary was by this unexpected gift. Rather than upset her, he kept his misgivings to himself.

Mary ran over to place the DVD in his hands. "You hold on to this, and I'll be right back. I'm adding popcorn and Skittles to the list so we can watch the movie in style."

Faelan looked up at her incredulously. "You do realize I'm a man."

"Oh baby, come on." She pouted prettily. "Watch it for your little subbie…"

"What do I get if I watch it?"

She gestured to the movie case, moving her hand up and down like Vanna White and stating in an announcer's voice, "If you watch this piece of American art with me, you will win free access to your subbie's body."

"I already get that as your Master," he answered drolly.

She leaned over him, whispering, "You can cross a hard limit."

He cocked his head. "Anything?"

Pressing against him, she answered, "Yes."

"Disney it is then."

Mary jumped up and down, giving him a quick peck on the cheek before running out the door. He had to admit, seeing this side of her was entertaining and sweet. Still…

Faelan looked at the colorful case with the dancing couple in the ballroom and shook his head. The man who left this on their doorstep was clearly sending a message. Somehow this stranger knew that this was Mary's favorite show, and that she was now residing here.

It didn't sit right with Faelan, but when Mary returned she was a bundle of childlike joy as she settled against him with her bowl of popcorn, and he couldn't help feeling differently. She was just too damn adorable like this.

"I can't believe it," Mary gushed. "I'm watching *Beauty and the Beast* in my home before everyone else sees the movie."

When she said the word *home*, Faelan suddenly felt more at ease. Mary was content here, something she had never experienced before. Was it possible his feelings of jealousy stemmed from the fact he was content as well and was simply afraid of losing this?

Wrapping his arm around Mary, he made the conscious decision to accept this mysterious gift and reap the rewards of it for himself. "Do you know what I am going to have you do for me?" he growled in her ear as the intro music filled the room.

She looked back at him, her eyes sparkling. "No. What?"

He walked his fingers slowly up her thigh. "Vanilla sex."

"No! You can't be serious."

Faelan bit her shoulder, causing goosebumps to cover her smooth skin. "Oh, but I am…"

Faelan had envisioned this encounter with Mary for years—ever since that night when she'd bared her soul to him, explaining how she'd lost her virginity as a young woman.

"You're telling me your father stole your innocence?" Faelan pressed when she shared the circumstances with him.

She glared. "That's not what I meant."

Faelan caressed her cheek, looking at Mary with compassion and tenderness. "I want to know what happened to you."

Mary growled. "It's not like he had sex with me, if that's what you're thinking."

"Okay…but a little explanation here would help."

Mary stared at him warily.

Faelan understood this was a rare opportunity being given to him, a gift of trust, and he took hold of her hand, meeting her gaze. "No judgments here. I only want to understand."

Her eyes softened. After several moments, Mary finally spoke. "My sixteenth birthday…"

Faelan felt his hackles instantly go up, his heart already breaking before she said another word.

"My father told me he was stopping me from ruining the life of another man—like my mother had." Her voice suddenly became distant, soulless. "The bastard tied me up like he had hundreds of times before, but…" She shook her head and looked down at the floor, her bottom lip trembling.

"What?" he asked gently.

Mary looked him dead in the eye. "That fucker used the handle of my mother's rolling pin so I could never use my virginity to 'enslave a man to hell'."

Faelan wrapped Mary in his arms, fighting the urge to punch something. She needed his compassion, not his justified anger.

Mary remained stiff and unyielding in his embrace, eventually pulling away. "It wasn't like it was sexual or anything."

"But he violated his own daughter—an innocent girl," he stated, his voice gruff with emotion.

"Innocent?" Mary's laughter was cold. "My mom was a cunt and my dad an abusive asshole. So what do you think that makes me?"

"A girl who endured hell."

Mary closed her eyes and shook her head. "Nope. I am a product of my heritage. That's why I will never have kids."

Faelan lifted her chin. "Mary, what they did…that's not on you, it's on them."

Mary shrugged and looked away.

He turned her head back and gazed into her eyes. "Only a woman with strength could survive what you did. But you didn't just survive, you overcame it. Graduating early to pursue a career as a pharmacist to help others—you did all that because it's who you are."

"I was such a fucking sap…"

Faelan grasped her chin and repeated, "*That* is who you are. Smart, uncompromising, and compassionate."

Mary laughed. "Compassionate, me? Hah! I would like you to find one other person who would call me that."

"Anyone who has ever received medication from your hand would say so. What else would you call a woman who chose her profession solely to protect people?"

"Foolish?" she suggested with a sarcastic grin.

"No, Mary." He cupped her face in both hands. "You lost connection to your truth because of your abusive upbringing. I want to help you reconnect."

Mary snorted dismissively. "What? Now you're my spiritual advisor?"

"I am your Dom—the man charged to guide and stand beside you."

Mary stared at him for a long time. "You don't know who I am."

"You're wrong. I see you very clearly." Faelan touched the center of her forehead with his fingertip. "It is you who can't see."

She shook her head and snarled, pushing away from him. "Don't you dare put me on a pedestal. I promise it will come crashing down on you."

"Mary, I see your flaws and…I get them. You don't need to hide anything from me. I accept and love you for who you are."

"Why do you do this, Faelan?"

"Do what?"

"Get all understanding and sweet on me? I need you to be a man who won't back down."

"That's exactly what I'm doing. I'm forcing you to face your biggest fear. As much as you say you want me to Dominate you, you fight me whenever it gets real."

"The fuck I do…"

"Do not mistake my acceptance of your flaws as weakness, Mary. I am not a lesser man for loving you. I am the only man strong enough to break through that impossible wall you have built around you."

"Fuck you! I don't need you to save me."

Faelan caressed her clenched jaw. "Trust that I know exactly what you need, and I will get you through to the other side."

"There you go again, getting all mushy on me," she complained.

The girl had been rejected, battered, and bruised, never knowing what it was to be truly loved. Faelan understood that about her, and unlike all the other men who had passed through Mary's life, he was determined to help her reconnect with the innocence that had been taken from her—stripped away by the very person who was supposed to protect it.

She had only known pain, using sheer grit and cold resentment to survive. He knew there were those close to him who questioned why he stayed loyal to her. Why put up with her constant outbursts and distrust?

But he was a man on a mission.

It had taken patience to wait until the timing was right. Tonight would bring to fruition what he'd envisioned for her that night two years ago.

"I will be collecting my debt after work."

"What? You expect me to get excited about vanilla sex with you?" she said with disinterest as she finished getting ready for work.

He planted a deep, possessive kiss on those teasing lips. "I will leave you breathless when I'm done."

"That's mighty big talk considering all the *things* we've done together."

"Just you wait," he answered with a wolfish grin. "There are clothes laid out for you on the bed for tonight. Follow the instructions and meet me at the designated location."

She gave him a quick peck on the lips, smiling. "What exactly are you up to, Mr. Wallace?"

He didn't answer as he put on his jacket and headed for the door.

"I hate vanilla you know," she said behind him.

He smiled to himself and turned to face her. "Come here."

Mary made her way to him, a smirk on her lips.

Placing his finger on those sarcastic lips, he commanded, "Trust me." He stroked the collar around her neck for emphasis.

She flashed him a look before darting her eyes to the floor.

"Where's the trust?" he insisted.

Mary took a deep breath, letting it out slowly before replying, "Fine. I concede."

He chuckled at her answer. "No. You must submit. There's a huge difference."

She pursed her lips, but eventually acquiesced. "I submit, Master."

"Good. After work you will cleanse your entire body and make it acceptable for sacrifice."

She flashed him a naughty smile. "Sacrifice? Now you're talking." She paused for a moment, visibly shivering. "I can't wait to see how this 'vanilla' night plays out…"

Faelan knew she would have hesitated had he shared his true intent—and he wasn't about to let Mary bolt.

As he guided her out the door ahead of him, Mary suddenly blurted, "Oh, I forgot something. Don't wait for me."

Faelan smiled as he left, knowing Mary would run to the bedroom to see what her instructions were. He'd kept them purposely vague.

The note read:

Dress with minimal makeup and your hair down. A cab will pick you up at 7:00. Everything I want you

to wear is in this box. No peeking until you get my text.

He laughed to himself. If she dared to peek, she would only find another note admonishing her for her disobedience.

There might be a spanking in your future if you fail to obey…

He looked back at the apartment, thinking of Mary with lustful amusement.

After Faelan finished his workday, he changed into the suit he'd stashed in the car. It was the same one he'd worn at the hospital when he'd collared Mary. He understood how close he'd been to losing her that day. Despite her fears, she'd knelt at his feet.

It was a significant commitment for both of them.

He wanted to remind Mary of her courage by wearing the suit tonight. Her trust then had meant everything to him, and this evening he would reward it.

Faelan gave the night manager instructions before heading out of the store, amid the whistles from some of the female cashiers who were appreciative of his more stylish attire. He never responded to their flirtations, but he certainly enjoyed the attention.

Easing into his cobalt Mustang, he revved the engine several times before heading out, feeling an incredible burst of energy anticipating what he had planned for the evening.

Faelan texted Mary, knowing she was headed home in LA traffic.

Your clothes are hanging behind the door in the

spare room.

It was a test.

Aren't they in the box? she typed back.

He smiled, gratified to know she had obeyed, although he was certain Mary had suffered the entire day wondering what the box contained. It was proof that she was making significant progress.

She would never see this coming…but he knew she was ready for it.

He sat at the bar waiting for Mary to enter the restaurant. He enjoyed the anticipation as he watched others come and go.

She arrived dressed in the simple black cocktail dress he'd picked out for her. It accented her striking blonde hair and shapely body. He watched with pride as several men turned to admire her.

Mary was a stunning beauty.

Faelan stood up and called out to her when it was obvious she didn't see him.

She turned her head with an amused smile on her face. "So, what's the idea behind my subdued getup? Minimal makeup and just look at these shoes." Mary lifted her exposed calf up to the delight of the men around her and pouted as she caressed the heel. "Four inches? You *know* I prefer six."

One of the men beside Faelan lifted his glass to his mouth, chuckling into his drink.

Fealan appreciated Mary's sexual reference and shot her a wicked grin, glancing down at his crotch. "Don't worry, doll. I've got what you need right here."

The other men watched her for a reaction. Mary fed on their attention and leaned over seductively, whispering loudly in his ear so they could hear, "Why don't we skip dinner so you can show me that bad boy?"

Faelan knew every man at the bar was wishing she were his date for the evening.

Too bad…

He took Mary's hand and kissed it, winking at her. "You'll need sustenance if you're to survive what I have planned tonight."

"Oh…" Mary purred. "I love the way you sweet-talk me."

Faelan nodded to the waiter to let him know they were ready. Placing his hand on the small of Mary's back, he guided her away from the hungry vultures and over to the private booth he'd reserved for them.

"Are we going to do it here?" Mary asked excitedly as she sat down.

"No," Faelan answered, taking out a thin wrapped box from his jacket and sliding it over to her. "A gift."

She laughed. "Oh, let me guess—a box of condoms."

"Open it."

Mary ripped at the paper and looked surprised to see a flat velvet box with a clasp. She held it in her hands and looked at him questioningly.

"Open," he commanded again with a charming smile.

Mary undid the clasped and lifted it slowly. She said nothing, a stunned expression on her face.

Faelan waited, in no hurry as she took it in.

Mary reached out to caress the necklace with a look of reverence.

"I remember you said it was your favorite."

She simply nodded, her eyes focused on the necklace.

"I bought it a few weeks ago in anticipation of the movie releasing on the big screen, but felt it was right to give it to you now. Would you like me to put it on for you?" he asked when she didn't respond.

"No. Not yet. I want to admire it a bit more."

Mary caressed the red ruby that represented the rose, then ran her fingers over the intricate mosaic of the Beast dancing with his beauty outlined in gold.

"I've never seen anything this beautiful before."

Faelan chuckled, pleased by her reaction. "Glad you like it."

"No," she stated, turning toward him. "You don't understand. This means more to me than you can ever know." Her bottom lip trembled as she looked down at the necklace.

Mary nodded as she stared down at it for several moments, seeming too moved to speak. Finally, she said, "No one has ever taken my love of Disney seriously—and my dad was brutal about it. But…that's because nobody understood that these movies saved my life when I was a kid. I needed to believe in magic and in a land far, far away. I lived the lives of every princess that came along, believing deep down that someday my prince would come. That belief was the only thing that kept me hanging on when I was ready to give up."

"I'm grateful they had that unique impact on you," Faelan said with sincerity, truly appreciating their significance in her life.

She gave him a wistful smile. "I never found out who sent me the movies, but the instant a new Disney movie came out, a copy of it would arrive on my doorstep. I always figured it had to be one of the neighbors, but no one ever 'fessed up."

"It let you know someone cared."

Tears welled up in her eyes. "Yep," she choked out.

"It became a lifeline back then."

Mary nodded, looking as if she were going to cry. "I can't tell you how many times I watched them all, but this one," she said, caressing the necklace again, "this one has always held a special place in my heart." She looked up at him, all sweet and vulnerable—a vision of the girl she'd been once. "Would you?" she asked, handing the necklace to him.

"Of course."

Faelan took it from her and fastened it around her neck, adjusting it so that it complemented her collar. He smiled at her with pride afterward. "Perfect."

Mary looked down at the necklace, unable to keep from touching the stones. "I've never seen anything this exquisite before."

"I didn't want to buy you simple costume jewelry, so I enlisted Celestia's help. She knows a few people in the fine jewelry business."

"Does she now?"

"She's friends with the artist who created this necklace, which is how I was able to purchase it for you. The man uses precious stones such as sapphire, emerald, amber, amethyst to create the mosaic." He shrugged and laughed. "Plus a few others I've never heard of."

"It's stunning. A real showstopper."

"Like you."

Mary looked up at him with tenderness. "I will never forget this, Faelan."

He leaned over to kiss her, but when he tried to pull away, she wrapped her arms around him, kissing him more deeply, confessing in a soft whisper, "I don't want this moment to end…"

"Lucky for you, the night is just beginning."

After dinner, Faelan surprised Mary by taking her to a dollar theater to watch the original Disney version of *Beauty and the Beast.* It was amusing sitting amongst a bunch of children, while they were dressed in their fine clothes. Mary totally ate it up, especially when some of the girls pointed to her and whispered something about a "princess".

Mary giggled—an actual giggle came out of her pretty mouth. Faelan shook his head, amazed at the magic spell this movie seemed to evoke.

Faelan spent the whole movie sitting back and observing Mary as she watched the show with rapt attention. It amused him that her lips moved throughout the movie as she mouthed every word. There was no doubt that the poor girl had truly watched that show hundreds of times. For some reason, instead of it becoming mind-numbingly boring to her, it only added to her adoration of it.

After the lights went up, the girls around her approached Mary and one was brave enough to ask, "Are you a princess?"

Faelan stepped in and answered for Mary. "Yes she is, but you have to keep it a secret." He put his finger to his lips. "If the enchantress finds out, she will turn my beautiful princess into a pill bottle. She works as a pharmacist, you see."

The girl nodded but looked at the others, unsure what to make of Faelan's answer.

The smallest one in the group piped up. "So does that mean you're her prince?"

Mary took over. "He's actually a big fluffy wolf, but was turned into a man to protect me."

The little girl walked up to Faelan and started petting him. "Nice puppy."

Faelan gave Mary a stern look, but then smiled down at the girl.

"What are you doing, Francesca? We don't touch strangers," a woman cried, grabbing the girl's hand. She looked up at Faelan and her voice caught for a moment.

"I…ah…sorry for my daughter's actions."

He grinned. "Not a problem."

The woman continued to stare at him as a blush slowly crept up her cheeks. He wondered if she'd recognized him from the documentary.

"Mommy, he's not a prince, he's a dog."

"Wolf, actually," Mary chimed in.

The woman shook her head, certain she hadn't heard clearly. "Anyway, we'd better be going…" She hurried off with her daughter trailing behind her. The little girl looked back as they left and waved as they made their way out.

"That was adorable," Mary exclaimed.

"What's adorable was watching you during the movie."

"Why?" she asked, sliding her arm around his.

"The way you react to everything…it makes me smile."

"As long as you're not laughing *at* me."

"Not at all." Faelan stopped in the middle of the theater hallway and turned to face her. "I love you."

She smiled, the kind of smile that reached all the way up into her eyes. "I love you, too."

He had to step back as a little kid ran between them and he laughed. "That's what I get for bringing you to a dollar theater."

Mary wrapped her arms around his waist, under his suit jacket. "I'm glad you brought me here. It makes me feel like a kid again, in the best way."

"Anything for you." He kissed her on the nose and guided her out of the noisy theater.

"So where to now?" she asked, swinging their hands as he walked her to the car.

"We' re headed home."

"Sacrifice…" she whispered, giving him a seductive smile.

"Sweet sacrifice," he answered.

"What does that mean?"

Faelan opened the car door, raising his eyebrow as he said, "Get in and find out."

Mary slid into the seat gracefully and looked up at him. "Even if it's lame, I want you to know everything so far makes up for it."

Faelan chuckled as he shut the door.

She still didn't trust him…

His Innocent

Once they arrived back at the apartment, he helped her out of the car and murmured in her ear, "I want you to imagine that you and I have only recently met and we've just ended our very vanilla date. I am inviting you inside because I'm really into you and I'm hoping you'll stay awhile."

"Well…you've gifted me with an expensive necklace and taken me to my favorite movie. I think the chances are you'll get what you want."

"Tonight it's not about what I want."

She looked at him strangely. "I thought you were crossing my hard limit tonight."

"I am. It's a one hundred percent vanilla scene."

"What about the sacrifice?" she pouted.

"It must be your choice."

"Of course, I'm all in."

He shook his head. "You must stay in character, Mary. I'm about to invite you in for a drink, but you have to decide if you'll let me take your virginity."

She almost rolled her eyes but stopped herself. "It's

pretty much a given. You know, jewelry, dinner…"

"But a woman like yourself isn't swayed by such things. You respond to the man, not the trappings."

"Huh, never looked at it that way before. Always been about the trappings for me…"

Faelan smiled as he guided her to the door. Once inside he asked her, "Would you like a mixed drink or some wine?"

"I'll have the usual." He went to get her rum and coke, but she stopped him. "On second thought, I'd like a glass of red wine. Please."

He nodded, grateful that she was falling into character.

He poured them both a glass and returned to her. He guided her to the sofa, but before he sat down he raised his glass. "Here's to a night with a beautiful woman."

She smiled and took a sip of her drink.

Sitting beside her, he began a light conversation. Treating the encounter exactly as he would have if they'd met in the vanilla world, he made simple physical gestures to let her know of his interest. A light "accidental" brush of hands, playing with a strand of her hair, pressing his thigh against hers, and looking deep into her eyes whenever she spoke.

He was pleased to see her respond naturally to those nonverbal cues, and as the night progressed the chemical attraction they'd always had for each other grew to a feverish pitch.

Faelan got up and poured the last of the wine before returning to her. "Would you be interested in going to the bedroom to make love?"

Mary lifted an eyebrow. "Possibly."

He smirked. "What would make that answer 'absolutely'?"

"I'd like you to kiss me the way you would make love to me."

Faelan's cock stirred hearing her request. He put down both of their glasses and moved closer to her. He clasped one hand behind her neck and used the other to cup her chin. Tilting her head slightly, he moved in.

He kissed her lips tenderly at first, building up the tension as they became more insistent, then he began tasting her lips with his tongue.

Mary moaned softly, relaxing in his arms as she gave in to his attention.

Faelan was purposely slow as he darted his tongue inside her mouth and slowly swirled his against hers. Her legs parted slightly, an instinctual reaction to her growing sexual need.

"You're so beautiful, Mary," he murmured as he moved to her shoulder and left a trail of kisses up to her neck.

Her breaths became increasingly shallow as he made slow, intimate love to her with his mouth—their clothes still on.

When he pulled away, she looked at him with those large, luminous eyes. "Wow...that was damn sexy."

He stood up and took her hand. When she grasped it, he smiled and pulled her up and into his arms.

She stared at him for several moments before saying, "I want you to make love to me, Todd."

He hadn't expected her to call him by his given

name. It gave him an odd thrill he wasn't expecting and made him desire her more.

Guiding her into his bedroom, Faelan instructed her to lie on the bed.

As she lay there looking up at him, his heart swelled with pride and longing for her. Vanilla or kinky, there was no doubt that Mary was a rare beauty.

All her hostile outbursts born of pain and self-loathing only made this moment that much sweeter. Before him lay a different woman. All the elements of Mary, but with an air of innocence and transparency.

It humbled him that she was willing to give this hidden part of herself to him.

Faelan undressed before her, his gaze locked on hers. He mentally separated himself from all their past memories, so that he could concentrate solely on the moment and the woman before him. It wasn't simply role play; this was entering into a brand-new connection with her.

He hoped she felt it too.

Keeping his boxers on, he joined her on the bed, lightly resting his hand on her stomach. He felt her tremble under his touch and knew she was now invested in this scene as much as he was.

He leaned forward, kissing her lips as he let his hands lightly caress her arm. This wasn't about satisfying his increasing libido; it was about making love to every part of Mary. Something he had never been allowed to do until now.

Mary seemed disconcerted by this new interaction, much like a woman introduced to BDSM for the first time. She was frightened and intrigued by the emotional connection it inspired, making her breath quick and her nipples hard against the material of her dress.

Faelan was both touched and saddened by that fact. The idea that a woman her age had no idea what it was like to simply be loved…it was a damn shame.

He began exploring her body, caressing her with her clothes still on. Gentle touches that became more exploratory as he slipped his hand up the skirt of her dress to graze her smooth thigh.

Mary positioned herself, subtly allowing him more access. His kisses became more passionate as his hand traveled farther up her leg and brushed the material of her lace panties.

She groaned in response, thrusting her tongue in his mouth, needing more connection. He focused on plundering her mouth as his finger snuck under her panties and he felt her wet pussy.

Oh, how it called to him.

Responding to that call, he moved down between her legs and eased her panties off. Putting his hand on her thighs, he spread them apart gently, exposing her bare mound with that tantalizing strip of blonde hair above her clit.

"I love a true blonde," he murmured as he lowered his mouth to take the first lick. Her pussy was swollen from the extensive time spent getting her to this point. It made her exceptionally tasty. Normally, he would have dived right in and left love bites along the way as he made her come.

This time he introduced her to his gentler side. Coaxing her erect clit to pulse with need as he teased it with his tongue.

"Please…" she begged.

Pulling back the hood of her clit, he began licking it at a slow, rhythmic pace, groaning as he did so. Bringing her to climax was pleasurable for him, and tonight it held more meaning.

I will love every part of this body tonight, he thought, smiling as her pussy stopped pulsing under his tongue for a moment just before orgasm.

He growled his satisfaction as she came against his tongue. After her climax subsided, he kissed each of her thighs before heading back up. He kissed her on the lips, sharing her juices with her—something they both got off on.

"You taste good," he murmured.

"I know," she answered, smiling as they kissed. "Why don't you take off these clothes now?"

"I was hoping you'd suggest that."

This demure side of Mary was a whole new experience. Even though she was a fully trained submissive and would do what he asked, she kept him on his toes trying to top him on occasion. It seemed a battle of wills for her, one that she wanted him to win, but couldn't allow without a fight.

He was certain it stemmed from her past and was the reason he was patient with her during those scenes when it was a struggle for her. He had no time for bratty subs who liked to dominate their Masters with their disobedience, but when it was a sincere attempt to please and struggle to get there, he would move heaven and earth to help his submissive achieve it.

Faelan crossed his arms behind his head and lay back to watch Mary undress before him. She did not do her typical striptease, but kept her eyes on him the entire time, her movements nervous as she fumbled with the zipper of her dress and the back of her bra.

Amusing that vanilla sex could cause this kind of response from her. He knew it was the emotional aspect that terrified her but, based on her hard nipples and swollen pussy, the challenge of it was enticing.

"Turn around for me," he stated as she stood in front of him completely naked.

Mary twirled around slowly, a shy look on her normally confident face.

"You have the body of a goddess and the face of an angel."

She tilted her head and smiled.

That look about did him in.

"Mary…" he called out to her.

She joined him back on the bed and he pulled her to him, closing his eyes as he held her tight. He imagined her pure and untouched, the woman she was—inside.

This would be her first night connecting with someone on both an emotional and physical level. Like a virgin, this was a brand-new experience for her ripe with all the tension and excitement it brings.

"My virgin beauty," Faelan whispered in her ear. "I want to make love to you."

Mary moaned softly, her body trembling under his touch.

Releasing his hold on her, Faelan removed his boxers, revealing the raging hard-on he had been suffering from since the very first kiss.

She looked down at his cock, then back at him and smiled.

"I love you," he told her. Lifting himself up, Faelan settled between her legs and braced himself with his arms to look down at her. "I have never loved anyone as much as I love you."

She bit her bottom lip and glanced away.

"Look at me," he commanded gently.

Mary turned her head back, tears in her eyes.

"Are you afraid?" he asked.

She nodded her head, her lip trembling. He could feel the well of emotions building up inside her, threatening to overwhelm Mary.

He smiled. "Don't be afraid, my beauty."

Her eyes softened, and she opened her legs wider as an invitation.

Grasping his cock firmly, he caressed her pussy with the head of his shaft, teasing her already sensitive clit.

Mary kept her eyes on him, holding her breath the moment his cock pressed against her opening. "I love you," he murmured huskily as his shaft slowly sank into her warm depths.

She didn't take a breath again until he was fully inside her.

Wrapping her arms around him, she pulled herself up and whispered in his ear, "I love you too."

Faelan closed his eyes. She had spoken those three words before, but this was the first time he'd felt them on a soul level.

In response, he began slowly stroking her with his cock, making love to her gently, tenderly. His hand ran over her bare skin as his lips sought out hers.

He tasted her tears and understood the source. She felt it too, this deeper connection that was otherworldly and eternal. It pulled at them both.

Mary's kisses became more intense and passionate, her need to be even closer driving her to wrap her legs around him and pull him in deeper. There was nothing in the world but the two of them. No past, no future—only now.

He held back for as long as he could, but eventually had to give in to the need for release. Grabbing her buttocks, he slid his cock deep into her, thrusting again and again. Mary lifted her hips and cried out in pleasure.

As they lay there afterward, Faelan felt the first telltale pulsations of her delayed orgasm just before her pussy began squeezing his shaft in rhythmic contractions. He kept still until the last wave had ended, then hugged her tighter before rolling off her.

In all his years, he had never experienced anything as intense.

Turning his head to look at her, Faelan caught Mary staring up at the ceiling.

"What are you thinking?"

She shook her head. "I never knew."

"Knew what?" he asked, brushing away a strand of hair from her sweaty cheek.

She turned her gaze on him and smiled. "It could feel like that."

"What? Vanilla sex?"

"No. Loving someone." She looked back up at the ceiling, a slight smile on her face. "No wonder people get all weird about it."

He brushed her cheek lightly with his thumb, a smirk on his lips. "I'm glad I could be your first."

She laughed, but suddenly stopped and looked at him. "Thank you for never giving up on me."

"I knew tonight would happen. I envisioned it way back at the Haven, the night you turned down Master O to scene with me. I thought all was lost when I got the news of my failing kidney—but I got my second chance and you came back to me. Ever since that day, I have been planning this night."

She shook her head in disbelief. "That long ago?"

"Yes. When I love someone, I love them completely."

She traced her finger over his lips. "You aren't like all the other boys, are you?"

"No. My loyalty is fierce." He grinned when he added, "Like a wolf."

"Awoooo…" she howled playfully.

Faelan grabbed her and bit down on her neck, announcing gruffly, "Mine."

Mary laughed as she settled into his arms. "I kinda like vanilla sex—in small doses, of course."

"Are you ready for round two then, kinky style?" he asked, nuzzling her ear.

"Please, Master."

With ease, they switched into their roles as Dominant and submissive and he had his way with her. Faelan noted a difference, feeling the love behind Mary's submission.

It charged him up and he experienced the most satisfying power exchange he'd ever had.

Dark Past

Their lives seemed to be settling into a comfortable routine after that night, enough that Mary braved broaching a subject Faelan refused to talk about with her.

There were parts of his past he kept hidden. He *had* shared a small portion of that history with Brie in hopes it might sway her to give him a chance after the collaring—it didn't.

As for Mary, he'd only made vague references to it if it might pertain to something she was suffering through. He'd kept that part of himself locked away from the world because it caused him only shame and regret.

The difference between Mary's tragic past and his was that she had been a victim, innocent of the crimes against her. He, on the other hand, was guilty of manslaughter, a crime that could never be undone.

Nothing he could do would ever change what happened that night ten years ago.

Faelan had been living in his silent hell for years—enduring the guilt of a survivor who should have been the one to die.

When Mary brought it up casually, he was unprepared. "Do you ever think about that boy who died in the car crash?"

For the first time he felt the impulse to unburden himself from the heavy weight. Rather than skirt the issue and redirect the conversation as he normally would, Faelan answered her frankly. "I think of Trevor every day." Saying his name out loud tore at Faelan's chest and he looked away from Mary. "I live with his death chained around me. The guilt I carry never leaves—not for a second."

"But why hang on to it after all these years?"

"It's not as if I have a choice, Mary. I stripped away his parents' hopes and dreams when I killed Trevor. They never had another child."

"It was an accident," she insisted. "It wasn't as if you set out to kill the boy."

"Lighting up a smoke while driving was dangerous. There's no excuse for it."

"Give me a break. People do it all the time."

"Just like texting on a cell phone, I know. But anything that distracts you while driving has the potential to kill someone. Hell, if I had wrapped my car around a tree, it would have been devastating to my parents, but at least it would have been fair. Killing someone else for your mistake is unforgiveable."

"I don't agree," Mary told him. "If people who make mistakes can't be forgiven, then what happens to all the shitheads in the world who purposely hurt someone? Are you saying they should get the death penalty?" She smiled to herself, mumbling, "I sure wouldn't mind seeing my dad bite the big one."

Faelan felt his stomach turn at Mary's statement. If there was a way to exact justice on her father, he would. But the man had disappeared after Mary graduated from high school. He up and left her, leaving his young daughter high and dry with no means of support. If Mary hadn't been intelligent and resourceful, who knows where she would have ended up. Truly, she was a hero in his eyes.

"I don't place judgments on anyone else—except your father. I would teach him about abusing little girls if I could." Faelan's blood began boiling as he envisioned that man tying Mary up to beat her repeatedly.

She shook her head. "We're not talking about me or my damn father right now. This is about you." She took his hand in hers and squeezed it gently. "I'm just saying it doesn't seem right that you should continue suffering because of something you did years ago. It was an accident. Why can't you let it go?"

He looked into her eyes, building up the courage to tell her the details about that terrible night…and the devastating consequences that followed. He hoped she would understand him without condemnation. The guilt he carried had influenced every aspect of his life, ever since that day he'd woken up in the hospital and found out Trevor had died in the crash.

"I'll tell you what happened, Mary. But you'd be the only one to hear the details. Brie knows only a few, I told Nosaka a little more, but other than those two I've kept my past closely guarded."

Mary nodded, a haunted look in her eyes. "I get it, Faelan. Talking about those moments with my father messes with my head."

"It's the same for me, but it would be a relief if someone knew everything and understood what makes me tick."

"I'm your girl," Mary assured him. "Hit me."

Going back to that time in his life brought up an excessive amount of pain he was hesitant to revisit, even now. He forged ahead despite his growing apprehension, hoping that sharing wouldn't resurrect the guilt he'd been trying to put behind him.

"Let me start before all of it happened." He looked at her and chuckled sadly. "I was a happy-go-lucky kid once, with a bright future and a harem of admiring girls at my beck and call."

"What? You telling me you were a rock star or something?"

He smirked. "Nah, can't play a lick of music, but I can handle a football like it was my bitch."

"You were a jock in high school?" Mary looked him over and nodded. "Yeah, I guess I can see that, but aren't you a little too scrawny to be a football player?"

"What I lacked in bulk I made up for in accuracy. Besides, being a quarterback takes more than just throwing skills. The leadership I brought got me on the varsity team in my sophomore year. I was the shit back then."

Mary raised an eyebrow. "The shit, huh?"

"Big shit." Faelan got up and pulled out his high school yearbook from his bookshelf. He handed it to her, not wanting to look, knowing Trevor's picture was in there. He said in a light tone to hide his growing unease, "My dad saw a bright future ahead for me. I had Oklahoma, Texas, and Florida in my sights after high school."

Mary flipped through the pages and stopped. A grin spread across her lips. "Oh, look at you. Quite the lady-killer, even back then. And that smile…" She looked up from the page. "I haven't ever seen you smile like that."

"That was a different life. I'm not that person."

Mary ran her fingers over the pages. "Well, I would have fucked this all-American boy and then shown him a thing or two in the process."

Faelan took the book from her and closed it. "Yeah, I bet you would have taught me a thing or two. My girlfriends back then were definitely vanilla."

"What was your family like? Not as shitty as mine, I take it."

"No, my parents were awesome back then. My dad believed in me and pushed me hard, but, rather than resenting it, I appreciated his support. As far as my mom, she had her hands full with my sister. Lisa was a problem child in middle school. Poor kid. She really struggled under my shadow and it infuriated her that her friends all flirted with me. I, myself, found it quite amusing."

"I bet." Mary smirked.

Faelan thought back on the kid he used to be, so confident with nothing standing in his way. How ironic that he was the one to ruin it. In one fell swoop, he became his own worst enemy—and an enemy of the entire town.

It was a long, hard fall to the bottom.

"The accident happened the night we'd won the game against our biggest rival. Man, that was some victory. One for the books. I was flying high because the state championship was in our sights. Clinching that win was a big deal, and the best part? I threw the winning pass. I remember Coach Clide slapping me on the back afterward and telling me, 'You're going to go far kid. Mark my words.'"

Faelan paused. Everything up to that point had been easy to talk about, but what came next was his living nightmare.

One he relived.

Every.

Damn.

Day.

"Don't hold back on me now, baby. I'm all ears," Mary encouraged.

Faelan braced himself for the emotions he was about to unleash. "I was a smoker, back when a sixteen-year-old could buy a pack. I thought it made me look older, which was important to the upperclassmen on the team."

"Never was tempted to try them myself. That shit kills."

The weight of his self-loathing increased with her statement, making it hard for him to continue. "Yeah…"

He was now regretting he'd started down this path with her but was committed. "I was flying high after pulling out that win and was speeding home to celebrate with my dad. I lit the cigarette without giving it a second thought, but the match fell between my legs. I totally freaked out trying to put the flame out."

Faelan stopped, tears forming in his eyes.

"Go on, baby."

"I was so busy swatting at the match, I never saw the car…" He swallowed hard as the vision of the crash played in his mind. "I looked up and realized I was in the other lane headed straight for it. The car might have tried to swerve out of the way, but there was no time to react. My headlights fell on the driver just before impact. I saw it was Trevor just before we hit." Faelan shook his head. "I will never forget the look of terror on his face."

Talking about it wasn't helping. The horror of that moment, the sound of the cars colliding, the acidic smell of the airbag exploding, and the sweet odor of radiator fluid mixing with burning oil—they all were etched in his mind.

However, it was the last moment of Trevor's life that Faelan could not let go of. That look of horror was how he would forever remember the boy.

It was his cross to bear.

"So you actually knew the kid?" Mary asked.

Faelan looked back at her. "We weren't friends. Well, at least not by that time. Trevor and I went to the same schools growing up. Early on in elementary school we started a club together, can't remember what the heck it was about though. We went our separate ways when I got involved in football. He wasn't the athletic type. Trevor was more of a brainiac. You know, the kind of guy who might cure cancer or something when he got older. I keep thinking about it."

"You can't know that."

"My only focus was playing football, but Trevor had bigger plans."

"How do you know?"

Faelan closed his eyes. "His parents told me."

"Oh God…"

"Yeah, it was bad. By the end, the whole town turned against me and I couldn't blame them."

Mary wrapped her arms around him, but he felt numb.

"What about your parents, didn't they defend you?"

"Yes, and by doing so they came under fire as well. My entire family suffered because of my mistake. It got so ugly, they were eventually forced to move. That's why my parents live in a cabin, alone in the mountains now. They left in shame for something I did. They didn't deserve that. Neither did my poor sister."

"Damn. How old were you again?"

"Sixteen."

"You were just a kid."

"So was Trevor."

"But it was a fucking *accident*."

Faelan rolled his eyes, knowing he was at fault and there were no excuses. "I was a new driver *and* I was speeding. I should never have been lighting up at the wheel. It was a fatal mistake that took Trevor's life."

"Shit, you really are fucked up."

"Too fucked up for you?"

"Hell no. But why have you let it mess with you so bad? Accidents happen. Life goes on."

"Yeah, my therapist tried to convince me of the same

thing. But she wasn't there. She didn't face the grief of Trevor's parents or watch my family go through hell because of it. I didn't ruin just one life, I destroyed two families that night."

"Fuck, I'm telling you, if my father felt one-tenth the remorse you do, I might be able to forgive him."

Faelan shook his head, not wanting forgiveness. "Remorse can't change the past."

"But it goes a hell of a long way in validating the person who was wronged. Seriously, it means something. It counts."

"It didn't for Trevor's parents."

"Did you personally ask for their forgiveness?"

He nodded. "I did, but I wish I hadn't. I only added fuel to the fire."

That haunting conversation sprang to his mind, tormenting him as he relived it.

"Can we see the boy?" a male voice asked just outside his hospital room. Faelan tensed.

"Let me ask him."

A nurse walked into Faelan's room and told him, "Trevor's parents are outside, Mr. Wallace. They would like to speak with you if you feel up to it."

Fear gripped his heart. How could he face them knowing he'd caused the crash that killed their son? He glanced warily at the doorway, but nodded his consent.

The two walked in, avoiding eye contact with him.

After the nurse left, however, the father shut the door and they both turned to face Faelan as one unit.

"Murderer."

Faelan looked at Trevor's mother, the guilt crippling him to the point he couldn't breathe as he listened to her. "My son should be alive, not you."

Lying in the hospital bed completely defenseless, having barely survived the accident himself, Faelan could do little else but take their wrath.

Tubes ran out in every direction and the pain in his side was excruciating. But nothing as painful as this. The anger and hatred in her eyes hurt far, far worse.

"I'm sorry..." he croaked, his whole body stiff and raw from the recent trauma.

"What good does 'sorry' do me when my son lies dead in the ground?" she demanded.

Trevor's father glared at Faelan with a dark, cold stare. "You stole our only son. There is nothing you can do or say that will ever atone for what you've done."

Still reeling from the fact he'd killed a person—someone he knew and had grown up with—Faelan said nothing.

Less than twenty-four hours ago he was throwing the winning pass and hailed the hero of the high school. Now he was a murderer.

"Why couldn't it have been you?" Trevor's mother cried, turning to her husband for solace.

"I—"

"I'm sorry to disturb you," the nurse interrupted as she opened the door. "It's time to check on my patient's vitals. Would you two mind stepping out for a bit?"

"We're done here," the father said. He pointed at Faelan. "I will tell the world what you've done. When I'm finished, you'll wish you were never born."

Trevor's parents exited the room, leaving their threat hanging over Faelan like a noose.

Putting her hand on his arm, the nurse tried to comfort him. "They're upset and grieving. Don't take what they say to heart."

"I killed their son." When he closed his eyes, he saw Trevor's face at the moment of impact. It jolted him physically. Then a new vision began to form. Trevor locked in a coffin, pounding against the lid in panic, begging to be let out.

"Are you okay?" she asked as she adjusted the tubing and had him lie back.

Tears came to his eyes when he confessed. "I should have died. The accident was my fault."

The nurse smiled kindly without judgment. "You survived for a reason. Embrace the gift and make the most of each day, for Trevor's sake and yours."

Faelan turned his head away from her, the words of Trevor's parents still ringing in his head. He knew with icy certainty that Trevor's father would follow through with his threat.

Mr. Fisher was a man of wealth and power.

"Like I said," Faelan sighed, looking back at Mary, "it didn't go well with Trevor's parents. My family paid the price, but it was my sister who truly suffered."

"Why, what happened to her?"

That was one subject he was not prepared to talk about and he suddenly regretted mentioning it to her. "We're done."

She gently grasped his arm. "Come on, Faelan. It's easy to tell whatever happened still eats you up inside."

Shaking his head, Faelan got up and walked away from her, needing to physically separate himself from the memories he'd just evoked. "Let it go, Mary."

She frowned, looking as if she was going to argue.

Faelan warned her not to push with a stern look.

Still wanting to force the issue, Mary remained silent but her thoughts were easy to read on her face.

There were times when it was important to tiptoe around her feelings, but this was not one of them. "Your thoughts speak for you and are the same as if you had said them aloud."

She opened her mouth to protest, but he held up his hand to stop her. "Don't make me regret having shared with you."

"My therapis—"

Failing to start her sentence with an apology was a serious error. It weakened his trust in her. Why would he ever choose to walk down that emotional road with her if she could not respect his limit now?

Faelan did not want this incident to define their future. He desired an open and trusting relationship. One where they both felt safe to share their darkest moments.

He *needed* to trust her.

Mary's willful disobedience when he had asked for

her understanding was disappointing. "You will go to the bed and kneel beside it until I call for you. Do you understand why you have earned this punishment?"

She let out a frustrated sigh. "I didn't listen to you."

"You did not. While I appreciate your concern for me, I know my own boundaries. I expected you to respect them, just as I have yours. Your total disregard for my feelings as well as my position as your Dom is deeply disappointing."

Mary wilted when he uttered those last words.

"Go now."

She bowed, saying quietly, "I'm sorry, Faelan."

"Those should have been the first words from your lips when I confronted you, but I accept your apology."

Mary walked off to begin her punishment. Rather than being upset, she seemed content. Fealan understood her well enough to know Mary needed the reassurance he was in charge whenever she overstepped. Had he let this slide, it would have undermined her confidence in him as well as his trust in her.

Being a Dom to a submissive like Mary was not easy, but he had learned to circumnavigate her many complexities.

Her Terms

Faelan should have known something was going to happen. He woke up feeling too happy, the kind of exuberance that seems out of place.

He didn't question it however. Opening the shower door, he joined Mary, ignoring the fact it would make them both late.

"Let me ravage this body of yours," he growled.

Picking up on his positive mood, she readily agreed. He ran his hands over her body, reveling in the firmness of her breasts and the roundness of those shapely buttocks. He slapped her ass, causing water droplets to fly.

Mary cried out in pleasure.

Pushing her against the cold tile, he grabbed her buttocks and spread her open, admiring the view of her pink outer walls and that hole that begged to be fucked. "We don't have time for more than a quickie," he explained, knowing their time was short.

"Exactly what I want," she purred. "Hurt me with that nasty cock."

"Hurt me, Master," he corrected.

She turned her head back and smiled mischievously, "Please, Master, hurt me with your hard, fucking cock."

With no warm-up, he shoved his rigid shaft into her tight pussy, then began pumping deeper into her. Biting down on her shoulder, he thrust harder as her body began coating him with her desire.

Faelan's growls became animalistic as he rammed into her body, focused on only one thing—coming inside that beautiful cunt.

Mary cried out in ecstasy, getting off on the rough sex. "Can I come?" she begged.

Wanting her to enjoy the morning jaunt as much as him, he readily agreed.

Mary snuck her hand between her legs and began rubbing her clit rapidly as he fucked her harder.

When the buildup had reached maximum intensity, he grabbed her hips and slammed into her. Mary screamed as she rubbed her clit more vigorously, wanting to come with him.

Faelan rammed her against the shower wall, forcing the last of his come deep inside her. He was pleased when he felt Mary's vaginal muscles begin milking his spent cock.

"Good girl," he growled.

Mary answered him with a loud moan, continuing her vigorous motion until the last of her pulsations ended.

As they were toweling off, Mary told him, "You haven't fucked me like that in a long time."

"I'm feeling in a particularly good mood today." He

ran his fingers over the scars on his abdomen. "It appears your nursing skills must be paying off."

Mary licked her lips as she stared at him lustfully. "I'm hoping to be treated in the same manner when I get home from work tonight. Maybe even a little rougher."

Faelan grabbed her wet hair and twisted it, pulling her head back. "You will get exactly what I want you to have."

Mary smiled up at him. "Yes, Master."

Faelan let her go and the two quickly got dressed for work. Grabbing nutrition bars for them both, he handed her one on their way out the door.

He didn't see the envelope lying on the doormat and would have passed over it if it hadn't been for Mary.

"Wait a sec…what's this?" she asked, bending down to pick it up. She looked to Faelan to see if he was playing a trick on her.

Faelan looked at the envelope with trepidation, a sense of foreboding settling over him as she turned it over and started to open it.

"It's not from me, Mary."

She stopped for a moment and then smiled even wider as she ripped the rest of the way and pulled out the notecard inside. "It has to be from my fairy godmother, don't you think?"

Faelan stared at the note, feeling violated by this unwanted intrusion.

Mary opened it up and began reading aloud. "Miss Wilson, I hope you have enjoyed my gifts through the years…" She looked up at Faelan, grinning. "I told you it was from her." She looked back down at the note and continued reading, "And now I would like to meet you in person. Please call me at your earliest convenience to arrange a date. I trust you won't mind flying to LA. Sincerely, Mr. Greg Holloway."

Mary stared at the familiar name, a stunned look on her face.

Faelan could not shake the growing feeling of dread. If he thought it would help, he would have torn that note from Mary's hands and ripped it into pieces. "Mr. Holloway. Is that the same man Brie has worked with in the past?"

Mary looked up from the note and nodded. "Brie always said the man had some kind of thing for me, but I just assumed…

"Assumed he didn't know you."

"Yeah. Never in a million years would I have guessed he was my secret benefactor."

"I question why he would want to reveal who he is now," Faelan told her.

"Beats me." Mary crumbled the note against her chest. "But how exciting is that? Instead of some old grandma lady, I have a famous producer wanting to meet me." Mary frowned. "I wonder what he wants?"

"I wonder that myself," Faelan said, taking the note from her to look at it himself. "I do not want you to call him."

"What? Are you kidding me!?"

"I don't trust the man. He knows you are a submissive, so if he wanted to meet you he should have approached me first. This is just odd and out of place," he stated, glancing at the note.

"Damn it, Faelan. Don't ruin this for me," she cried.

He furrowed his brow, now even more concerned. "What do you mean 'don't ruin this'? You know the protocol. If this man is serious about meeting you, he should contact me. I *am* your Master."

Mary's eyes remained glued on the note he held. "But I want to meet him."

"I'm not denying you that, Mary. I simply expect him to follow protocol."

She growled under her breath. "Fine."

Faelan folded the note and slipped it into his pocket. "Let's get out of here so we aren't more late for work."

He could feel Mary's irritation as they headed to their separate cars. It did not help her cause. He was not going to budge on this. If Mr. Holloway insisted on thwarting protocol, Faelan would be obligated to inform the BDSM community in Los Angeles. Famous or not, no Dom had the right to pursue a collared sub.

Mary changed after that day, becoming silent and sullen. He could feel her pulling away and was desperate to stop it.

Even though he normally kept his private affairs to himself, he decided to share his concerns with Tono Nosaka. The Kinbaku Master had arranged weekly meetings with him after Faelan had recovered from the transplant surgery. Although Faelan had initially been resistant to the idea, certain Nosaka would use that time to lecture him, he soon began looking forward to their meetings.

It turned out he'd been wrong about Nosaka. The guy might be old-fashioned in many respects, but he was still someone Faelan could relate to. It didn't hurt that he had a part of the man living inside him—a kidney—which inspired a feeling of brotherhood between them.

"What's wrong, Todd? You seem burdened today," Nosaka observed when Faelan sat down.

He gave the man a sideways look before choosing to tell Nosaka the truth. "I'm losing her."

Saying the words out loud sent a chill down his spine.

"Has something happened? I know Mary has struggled before with the idea of being collared."

"You mean when she talked to Brie and Lea on the phone and then complained that she didn't get to play with the Russian?"

Nosaka nodded.

"I had no problems with it, and would actually enjoy watching them together. I planned to approach Durov the next time he came to the States and told her so. I get that she's a free spirit. It's never bothered me."

"So what's changed?"

"Someone from her past has made his presence known. He wishes to meet her in LA. He is part of the community there and tracked her down to my apartment in Denver, but did not have the decency to speak to me first."

"Is he someone I know?" Nosaka asked.

"Yeah, it's that guy, Greg Holloway."

"Brie's producer?"

"One and the same," Faelan growled angrily.

"What possible connection could he have with Mary?"

"Truthfully, that remains a mystery. All I really know is that he left her gifts on her doorstep as a child. It was a kind gesture in a cruel situation, but it ended when she graduated from high school. Why he has tracked her down now makes no sense to me."

"That is quite odd," Nosaka agreed.

"I have to assume he plans to pursue her since he left me out of the picture."

"That may not be the case."

Faelan raised an eyebrow. "Brie told Mary that the old guy has had a thing for her since the beginning. He was the one who insisted Mary be in both documentaries and asked personal questions about her during their meetings."

Nosaka sat back in his chair. "Now that puts a whole different spin on it."

Faelan snarled. "He is a respected man in the community, yet he is knowingly breaking protocol by contacting her directly. And I can only speculate what it is he wants to do with her at that meeting."

When Nosaka reached out his hand, grasping Faelan's shoulder, he found the firm grip calming.

"Is Mary set on meeting with him?" Nosaka asked.

"She is."

"You are right to insist he speak to you directly. Have you considered contacting him yourself?"

Faelan frowned when he answered, "I did. The dick

treated me as if I were a messenger boy, not her Dominant. He wouldn't answer any of my questions and instructed me to have Mary call him personally."

"That does not sound like a healthy situation."

"I totally agree, but Mary doesn't see it that way. This is the person who helped her survive her childhood abuse with those small gifts. She feels the man saved her life and she wants to thank him for it."

"Couldn't her gratitude be expressed in a letter or a video?"

Shaking his head, Faelan huffed. "She insists it must be in person."

Nosaka picked up his cup of tea and took a sip before responding. "Mr. Holloway's dismissive attitude toward you is disturbing. The fact Mary is not upset by his treatment of her Master says a lot about her state of mind right now."

Faelan closed his eyes. The writing was on the wall. He was going to lose her no matter what he did. Let her go, and he was certain the producer would seduce her with his power and money. The fact Holloway refused to have the meeting with Faelan present left him no choice but to deny the encounter.

Opening his eyes again, Faelan admitted, "The tension of the situation is causing animosity between us."

Nosaka looked at him with compassion.

"Mary claims she feels trapped, but I have done everything in my power to support her without compromising us as a couple."

"You have been exceedingly thoughtful in your care of her and the situation."

Tears came to Faelan's eyes. "I love her."

Nosaka nodded, his eyes reflecting a similar pain. "We do not choose who we love, but we do choose *how* we love."

Faelan groaned. "I don't want to be relegated to friend status again. She and I have come so far, to go backward now…" He looked at Nosaka. "We were happy together."

Nosaka nodded in agreement, but reminded him, "We both know Mary carries wounds that still influence her rational thought. She comes from a place of need. It colors her decisions, as well as the way she views the world."

"Is there nothing I can do?"

"I would tell Mary exactly how you feel. Be completely open and honest with her, put everything on the table. Mary is at a crossroads. She must choose her future, and it is imperative that decision be based on truth."

"I don't want to lose her," Faelan stated, his stomach turning in knots.

Nosaka was empathetic. "You have provided her a safe and loving environment. There is nothing more you can do as a Dominant. Unfortunately, her ultimate decision is out of your hands."

"I can't handle it if she runs. I won't!"

Nosaka looked at him kindly. "We can't hold on to what was never ours. You *will* survive whatever decision Mary makes. If you are meant to share this life together, this test will bring you closer together. If not, you will be set free. You will need to think of it that way."

"I will never love again if that happens."

"I know it feels that way now, but we can't know what the future holds."

Faelan stared hard at Nosaka. "I won't *ever* put my heart on the line again if she leaves me."

"Do you regret collaring her?"

Faelan was taken aback by the question and frowned. "No…but I went into it believing we had a future together."

"Most people have their hearts broken multiple times in this life. It's human nature to want to protect ourselves from the pain, but it limits our experience on this Earth—not enhances it. I would rather know pain and *live* than isolate myself and feel nothing."

"You are a braver man than I."

"I disagree," Tono replied with a smile. "I see a strength in you I admire. It was forged in the past but continues to increase over time." Faelan felt a quickening in his spirit, as if Nosaka was speaking to something much deeper. "You will come out of this stronger, whichever way it goes. Trust that, and move forward with conviction, Todd Wallace."

Faelan shook his head. "I don't know how you do it."

"Do what?"

"Make me feel okay about an impending heartbreak."

"You are destined for great things. Whether it is with Mary by your side or not, your path has not changed."

"You know, I really couldn't stand you when we were fighting for Brie. I resented you even more when I found out you were my donor. But damn, Nosaka, you are an extraordinary human being. I mean that."

Nosaka looked down at his tea and smiled. "I found your arrogance off-putting when we first met. I won't deny it. However, your need for a transplant was a turning point for both of us. Fate was kind setting our paths to intersect."

"I'm alive because of it."

"And I am a better man for it," Nosaka countered.

"I don't think I ever told you how much I look forward to these weekly get-togethers. Although I was initially reluctant, I have come to count on these talks."

"As have I."

Faelan looked down at his empty coffee cup. "I guess that's it then. Tonight, I will either have the answer I want from Mary or…"

"You will be a free man," Tono finished.

Faelan entered the apartment feeling less conflicted than when he'd left. It gave him the courage to have a deep conversation with Mary—but she never gave him the chance.

Mary's expression was icy and hostile when she turned to face him. "I'm done."

She said it with such finality that Faelan held his breath.

Moving over to her, he took Mary in his arms, wanting desperately to break through this stone wall she'd erected. "I know we've been struggling lately, but we can work through this."

When she stared into his eyes, he felt a sense of panic wash over him. Her eyes held a coldness he hadn't seen in all the years he'd known her. "Don't do anything you'll regret," he warned.

"This moment has been coming for a long time."

"Why? Because some stranger wants to come between us?"

"Why couldn't you just let me go, Faelan?"

"You know why."

"No, I'm not talking about Mr. Holloway. I mean after you left me at the commune. You should have kept going. You should never have collared me. You know it and I know it."

"I didn't come running back. You came to me."

Mary's nose crinkled into a snarl. "Because of that damn Brie. She just had to butt her nose in my business."

Faelan lifted her chin, although Mary resisted. He forced her to look into his eyes. "It wasn't Brie's fault and you know it."

"The fuck it wasn't!"

"You knew that by telling Brie how you felt, I would eventually find out. She was only a pawn in your game."

Mary ripped herself from his grasp and moved toward the window. "You have no idea what you're talking about."

"Mary, I know you so well. I feel the unspoken anger and fear you carry inside you even now. I am not scared or offended by it. I want to help."

She whipped around and yelled at him. "Stop being so damn perfect. I'm so sick of it!"

"What do you want me to do? Tie you up and beat you like your father?" he growled. "Are we really back to that after all we've been through?"

Mary rolled her eyes. "Oh, I've never fucking asked you to love me. I never wanted it."

"Bullshit. You wanted me at your graduation and you pursued me relentlessly until I finally got the hint."

"Yes, I wanted you, but only to play with. You knew I abhorred commitment."

Faelan moved away, her resentment causing his own blood to boil. "You say you don't want commitment, but it is the only thing you truly crave. You never got it from your mother or father, not because you weren't worthy but because they were incapable of it."

"Well then, that's me. I'm their fucking offspring after all. What do you expect?"

He faced her as he said emphatically, "You *are* different from them. I see you for who you really are and that frightens you."

"Pah-leese… What I *know* is I feel suffocated whenever I am around you. It's like I can't breathe."

"If you need time away, take it. There's no reason to ruin what we have because you're running scared right now."

"Damn you!" she screeched. "You refused to listen, so let me make this perfectly clear. I don't want this. I don't want you!"

The icy dagger of her words penetrated his heart and left him momentarily stunned.

"You knew who I was when you collared me. It was always going to end like this. You know that. I can't stand being caged, and you telling me to take some time off totally infuriates me. I can't even have the satisfaction of leaving you because you are 'allowing' me to do it. Well, fuck you!"

Faelan shook his head helplessly as he watched his whole world crumbling before him.

"You became a total pussy the night you killed that boy. All these years you've blamed yourself and let life walk over you. Even now, you're looking at me like a lost puppy. Well, I'm not your goddamn savior."

"No, you're not. I'm yours."

Mary blew up. "And there we have it! Lord Faelan, self-appointed savior of the damned." She smiled cruelly. "But you had no idea who you were messing with when you fell in love with this damned soul, did you?" She leaned forward, beckoning him closer. "I'll let you in on a little secret…"

Faelan stayed where he was, glaring at her as he prepared his heart for her final blow.

"I've been playing you this whole time. I knew you would fall in love with me, all men do. I also knew you would ask for me back. I played with your feelings like a cat plays with a mouse before it pounces for the kill. I knew I would crush it into a million bloody pieces someday. I warned you plenty of times."

Coldness took over Faelan's heart, but the fighter in him had to tell her the truth. "You are only fooling yourself if you think that."

Mary's laughter was ruthless and cruel. "Why did you

trust me with your heart? You knew I would destroy it."

"No," he said, his voice strained. "What you are doing is killing your one chance at happiness. I see it clear as day, don't you?"

"You called this happiness?"

"It could have been if you'd given us a chance."

"Your love suffocates me."

"Only because it's real and you can't handle it."

"Shut the fuck up."

"You only talk like that when you know I'm right."

She glared at him.

"No one will ever love you like I loved you."

Mary sneered. "Well, I don't need the love of a boy. I need a man."

"You'll get exactly what you deserve, Mary. But I wanted so much more for you."

"Spare me your sympathy."

Faelan stepped back from her. He looked at Mary with a critical eye as if for the first time. She had everything going for her, the looks, the smarts, the talent, and the drive. But she lacked one critical element. She didn't believe her own worth, and no amount of love from him would ever change that.

He understood that now…

Faelan closed his eyes and turned away from her.

"Just so we're clear, I'm walking out on my *own* fucking terms."

"Go," he said under his breath.

"On my terms!" she screamed as she walked to the bedroom and started ripping her clothes off the hangers, throwing them onto the bed.

Faelan walked out of the apartment, feeling completely cold to his core. He wandered the streets in a daze, oblivious to where he was or where he was going.

Sure, he'd noticed her pulling away months ago, but he had believed, with time and patience, he could prevent this from happening.

Tono Nosaka had prepared him for the eventual break, convincing Faelan that it was time to let Mary go, but he couldn't give up on her. Faelan knew the trapped soul inside that smugly confident façade she wore like a shield.

Mary was right, however. He truly believed he was the one to save her. He endured all those trials she'd put him through. And now she'd proved him wrong. Pulling out his phone, he dialed Captain's number.

"Just a heads-up. Mary left me. I have to assume she'll be heading to LA soon and she'll need your guidance."

Captain cleared his throat. "I'm sorry it has ended this way."

"Not looking for sympathy, but wanted you to know. She'll need someone by her side when she finally crashes. Not that she'll ask for help from anyone."

"I will inform Dr. Reinstrum and see what he advises I do." Captain paused for a moment before asking, "Are you okay?"

"No, but I'll survive."

"I may be close to Mary, but I consider you a friend as well. If you need anything, don't hesitate to call. Candy and I both admire your loyalty toward *lief*."

"Unfortunately, it didn't win me any favors with her.

Quite the opposite. I'm just an idiot who had his heart ripped into shreds for her entertainment. Everyone saw it coming—but me."

"Mr. Wallace, your loyalty toward *lief* and your respect for her has been deeply appreciated. For that, you have my highest regard."

"Thank you but, to be honest, I'm feeling pretty stupid right now."

"Never regret being a good man."

Faelan closed his eyes as he hung up the phone and the numbness began to fade as the pain set in.

He'd lost her…

The thought of never hearing her soft laughter as she lay in his arms, the look of open trust in those eyes, or the feel of her sensual lips against his was crushing to his soul. They'd made such progress—as individuals and as a couple. It seemed unreal to him that it was over after everything they'd been through.

Over.

That word rang in his head with the heavy weight of finality.

Faelan took his time walking back to the apartment. Cold silence met him as he entered the place. He walked directly to the bedroom to confirm what he already knew. All her things were gone, except one. In the trash he found the collar he'd given her.

Faelan's breath caught as he reached down to pick it up, holding the symbol of her commitment in his shaking hand. It was like a second death, losing the future he thought they would have together—knowing she never wanted it.

He carefully placed the collar on the dresser, fighting back tears.

Looking around his place, Faelan realized he couldn't stay here anymore. There were too many memories that centered around her.

Heading to the bed, he lay down and closed his eyes, trying not to let the silence overwhelm him.

It's time to go.

Just like Master Anderson, he felt his time in Colorado was drawing to a close. He knew his parents would not take the news lightly, or his sister…with her new baby.

Uncle Todd would soon become a distant memory for the little guy.

"But damn, there's no point living with regret," he said aloud in his quiet apartment. He'd lived too much of his life in the shadows of mistakes from his past. It was time to take control and make it a life he wanted to wake up to every day.

He owed that to Trevor—and himself.

Faelan resented the unwanted intrusion when his phone started to ring and he saw the name Marquis Gray pop up on the screen. "Hello?" he answered hesitantly, unhappy the news of their breakup had already spread among the group.

Damn that Mary…

"Mr. Wallace, you've come to my mind several times today, prompting this call."

"Odd."

"That I'm calling or that you came to mind?"

"Both."

"I trust my mental impressions and always act on them."

Faelan said nothing, hoping he could navigate the conversation without having to address the breakup so soon—his emotions still too fresh.

Marquis let the silence drag for several seconds before stating, "Are you going to tell me what's wrong or do you prefer to dance around the issue?"

Faelan swept his hair back, laughing uncomfortably as he lay back down on his bed and closed his eyes. There was no getting out of this.

"So, I take it you heard what happened today."

"No, I simply had a sense something was wrong."

It was uncanny how well Marquis could read people, even when huge distances separated them. "What do you mean?" Faelan asked, still hoping to skirt the issue.

"I'm sensitive where my intuition is concerned and have learned to trust it completely," Marquis explained. "I believe it is how God speaks to me, but many prefer to call it a sixth sense."

"Whatever it is, you have a frightening power. You know that, don't you?"

"Only if I were to use it for evil," Marquis answered. "But I take the gift entrusted to me very seriously and do not abuse it."

"I suppose there's no avoiding this, then."

"I only wish to help," Marquis assured him.

Faelan let out a long sigh, wishing he could crawl into a hole and disappear. "I'm sure it will come as no surprise…" he began, but the lump in his throat prevented him from saying more, so he swallowed it down and forced out the words. "Mary's gone."

The silence on the other end was long and excruciating to bear.

Finally, Marquis spoke. "I am sorry to hear that."

"I'm certain you saw this coming, like everyone else, but I believed Mary could break away from the demons of her past. We were so close…"

"She wasn't ready."

Faelan's heart sank, knowing it was true. He had forced her into accepting his collar.

"Your transplant forced a situation she was unprepared for."

"She did want to run," Faelan admitted, thinking back on that day.

"But her love for you caused her to stay."

Faelan laughed angrily. "She doesn't love me. Never did."

"You know that's not true."

"Hah! You weren't there. You didn't hear the shit she spewed today."

"I suspect the more normal things became between you, the more frightened she became."

Faelan felt a check in his spirit. "Go on…"

"She still has multiple issues to work through. She not only needs professional help but more time to heal."

"Well, after what happened between us today, I'm done."

"As you should be."

Faelan snorted. "I was halfway expecting you to convince me not to give up on her."

"When your partner begins to undermine your respect, there must be a cutoff point. It makes no sense to sacrifice one partner over the other. Both must flourish for it to be a viable relationship."

"Agreed. You should know something, however."

"What's that?"

"Your friend, Mr. Holloway, instigated what happened today."

The tone in Marquis's voice was somber. "How was he involved?"

"He has been a part of Mary's life since she was a child, but no one knew. He kept his identity hidden—until now. When I demanded he go through me to meet with her, all hell broke loose."

"This is extremely disheartening," Marquis stated. "I will speak to Greg personally."

"It won't change things."

"No, but you deserve an explanation, as well as an apology from him."

Faelan felt slightly vindicated. "Thank you."

"So let me ask, how are you feeling about your future now that this has happened?"

Faelan assumed that Marquis's concern came from how he'd struggled when Brie had chosen Davis. "I've just made the decision to leave Colorado."

"Do you know yet where you will be going?"

Faelan laughed. "I'm sure you will advise otherwise, but I was considering heading back to LA. I had a good thing going before I hooked up with Mary and headed to the commune in Montana. I'd like to see if I can rebuild what I had at the Haven."

"I think that's an excellent idea."

"Again, you surprise me."

"Why would that surprise you? You are well respected here and have much to contribute to our community. Both Celestia and I would welcome your return."

Faelan was surprised to hear he felt that way, especially when Faelan held Marquis in such high esteem.

"When should we expect to see you then?"

"I'm certain my old company in LA will take me back, but it'll take me a while to find an apartment. You know how it is in California, and I'm strapped for cash as it is."

"I will need to discuss it with Celestia, but let me suggest you consider staying with us while you look for a place. It's much easier to find an apartment when you are already in LA. As you know, most apartments are rented before they ever show up on the internet."

"Oh hell, I remember. Decent apartments get snatched up as soon as the rent sign goes in the window."

"Please consider my offer, then. I have something else I would like to discuss with you, but it can wait until you arrive."

Faelan looked around his bedroom with a sense of relief knowing he wouldn't have to remain here much longer. "Hey, thanks for the offer, Marquis. I believe I may take you up on it if Celestia is agreeable, and I'd pay rent as soon as I get my first paycheck."

"It would be preferable if you pay us after you have secured an apartment and have the proper amount for the deposit. No rush."

Faelan was gripped by a sense of overwhelming gratitude, and had to rein it in so he didn't sound like a babbling idiot. "You know…I didn't want to speak to anyone when the phone rang, but I'm glad you listened to that sixth sense."

"I am too, Mr. Wallace."

"Hey, it's fine with me if you call me Todd. Mr. Wallace seems so formal when I'm going to be rooming with you."

Marquis cleared his throat, seeming surprised by the request. "Well…if that's the case, you can call me Ash whenever we're in private. The name is short for Asher. As the eighth child of a religious family, my parents decided to give me a biblical name and chose the eighth son of Jacob. Being a rebel at heart, I insisted everyone call me Ash when I turned ten."

Faelan laughed. "I can't imagine what it must have been like for your parents raising you."

"They would say it was a struggle, no doubt."

It seemed odd to call the great Marquis Gray "Ash", but Faelan appreciated the huge honor he'd been given. Ever since he'd known the Dom, the man had only been addressed as Marquis Gray and nothing else. Faelan wondered how many other people had been afforded the same privilege.

"Let me know if Celestia is opposed to my coming, otherwise I will begin my extraction from Denver immediately."

"I will speak to her as soon as I end this call. If you do not hear from me, you can assume she welcomes you as well."

"Thank you, Ash," Faelan replied. "Thanks for both the call and your generous offer."

"My pleasure, Todd."

"I'll keep in touch and give you a date when I have one."

"Good. Until we speak again."

Faelan hung up and stared at his phone, completely stunned.

A few minutes ago he'd been facing one of the darkest moments in his life. Now he was headed to LA to stay with the notorious Marquis Gray. The wealth of knowledge the man held was unfathomable, and he'd mentioned wanting to talk to Faelan about something else.

What that could be, Faelan could only imagine.

Funny how life unfolded. Every time one door closed another opened, taking him in a completely different direction.

He'd been looking to settle down and start a life with Mary. He'd fought tooth and nail to achieve that goal—and failed.

Now a whole new world of opportunity was opening up.

It was impossible to feel discouraged when he had the support and encouragement of Marquis.

Now the difficult task of saying good-bye lay ahead of him. He would have to keep his feelings of elation to himself, knowing his family would not understand or appreciate them.

His gaze fell back on the collar sitting on the dresser as Nosaka's parting words came to mind.

"Thank you, Mary," he muttered out loud.

You've set us both free.

Turning the Page

Faelan met with his family for a meal. He figured having them gathered together would make the news easier for them to swallow, but he hadn't counted on how hard his sister would take it.

"So, big brother, finally spending time with your own family, are you?"

"Hush, dear," his mother scolded. "Give the poor kid a break."

Lisa grumbled, "Todd ain't no kid, Ma. And he has his uncle duties to attend to."

Faelan glanced at the little tyke with a twinge of guilt. He could already tell this wasn't going to go well today and considered bailing.

Lisa looked at Faelan critically, then narrowed her eyes. "What's wrong?"

"Why does something have to be wrong?" he answered evasively.

"Well, the most obvious—your girlfriend's not here. And, to tell the truth, you're not looking so good."

"Don't give Todd a hard time," his mom reprimanded. "You know very well he's still recovering from the surgery. And there's nothing wrong with my son wanting to visit his mama without his girl. It's actually sweet."

Leave it to Lisa to see the truth and his mother to ignore it, using it instead as an excuse to baby him.

"Lisa is right," Faelan stated, deciding that jumping all in was better than sitting here the entire evening waiting for the right moment to drop the bomb.

Giving his dad a friendly slug to his shoulder, he said, "Turns out I'm on my own again."

His mother stopped setting the table and cried, "What?"

"What the heck did you do to Mary?" Lisa accused.

His dad was the only one to show any empathy. "I'm sorry to hear that, son."

Faelan nodded to his father, grateful for the simple words. He was missing Mary fiercely, and rational thought did not sway his freshly broken heart.

"Son?" his mother whimpered.

Faelan faced his sister and his mother and answered their questioning faces with the humiliating truth. "Mary left me. There's really not much more to say on the matter."

"But why would she do this to you?" his mother questioned. "She seems like such a nice girl."

Lisa glanced at him warily, as if she already knew he was leaving. "You okay, big brother?"

He looked her in the eye, shaking his head.

Lisa picked up her son, hiking him on her hip, and moved over to Faelan. "You're not running away again. You wouldn't do that to little Joshua? To me?"

"Sis, I—"

Tears came to Lisa's eyes. "You can't do this to me again! I *need* my big brother."

"I know you want me to stay, but I can't."

His mother gasped, suddenly understanding. "You're leaving Colorado?"

Faelan hated seeing the disappointment in their eyes, knowing he was the cause.

"Why are you doing this to us?" Lisa demanded. "Don't you owe this family something? After everything we've gone through?"

Faelan grabbed the back of the chair beside him, physically rocked by her words. He remembered all too well walking in on Lisa that day when she almost…

What almost happened was something the two of them never talked about. A heavily guarded secret.

Something their parents didn't even know.

His father spoke up. "Don't start on him, Lisa. Your brother just had his heart broken."

"What about me?" she cried. "When do my feelings ever count in this family?"

His mother rushed over to her and began stroking her hair, cooing, "There, there…this is a terrible shock for all of us."

Lisa glared at Faelan. "You're always hurting this family, damn it. Haven't we been through enough for you? I just want normal!" Her son began to cry so she left the room with her husband trailing behind her.

"Give her time," his father stated, a look of concern on his face.

"Todd, honey, please don't leave us," his mother

begged, grasping his arm tightly. "How will I know you're okay?"

He stared at his mother, feeling an overwhelming sense of guilt seeing the lines of worry that covered her face and the gray hairs peppering her once-chestnut hair. They were there prematurely—because of him.

"I'll do a better job of calling, Mom," he promised.

"Ada, we can't keep our son tied down. He's a man for Christ's sake," his father declared.

Lisa came back into the room without the child or her husband in tow. "Joshua doesn't need to see me fighting with you. In fact, he doesn't need to see you at all since you won't exist once you go."

Faelan frowned, not liking that possibility. "I won't let that happen."

"Oh yeah," she said, putting her hands on her hips. "Tell me how since you're running out on us."

"Like I just promised Mom, I'll call you guys once a week. Maybe even video chat. That way I can see Joshua grow up and maybe he'll recognize me when I visit."

Lisa huffed. "I can count the number of times you visited on one hand."

"It doesn't have to be one way. I'm going to be looking for a place nearer to the beach. Wouldn't that be fun? I'll introduce Joshua to the ocean and show you guys a great time when you come. I'm sure it'll help with my favorite uncle status."

Lisa gave him a droll smile, stating sarcastically, "Since you're his only uncle, that's not saying much, now is it?"

"Lees, you gotta understand." He chose to call her

by his shortened name for her, hoping it might ease the tension and allow her to *hear* him. "Staying would only be for you guys. There is nothing for me here except bad memories."

"I wish we were enough…" she muttered under her breath.

Of everyone here, his sister had paid the biggest price for his mistake. It had almost cost Lisa her life. He owed her, but staying wasn't an option.

"Hey, maybe I'll become famous and we can all live on the beach," he joked, hoping she'd let him go.

"What? You planning on becoming a big porn star in Hollywood now that you did that kinky documentary?"

"Lisa!" her mother cried.

"No, sis. My plans are much, much higher than that," Faelan replied with a smirk, trying to defuse the situation with misplaced humor.

His father shifted uncomfortably where he sat, the whole Dominant thing a bit too deviant for his Baptist background. "Do we really need to go there? Suffice to say, Todd had his heart broken by a beautiful girl." He looked at his son. "And I will miss the girl."

"Me too," his mother piped in. "I really liked Mary."

Faelan closed his eyes, trying to keep his emotions at bay.

His father uttered, "But facts are facts. She's gone, and soon you will be too."

Faelan stared at his father, the reality of the disappointment he must be to the old man weighing on him. To go from having a son who was a star quarterback to a gypsy with no career path or any notable accomplishment other than his ties to kink... What father could be proud of a son like that? "You know I'm sorry, Pop. For...everything."

His father grabbed him by the back of the neck, pulling him within inches of his face. "Only thing I want for you, son, is to keep fighting. As long as I know you're fighting, I don't have to worry about you." He let go of Faelan and looked at his wife. "Isn't that right, Ada?"

She glanced up at him, trying to hide the tears in her eyes. "Todd...I don't care what you do, I just want you to be happy. It's what every mother wants for her child. I hate that you've suffered more than most. I want you to get your time in the sun."

"What about me?" Lisa demanded. "Don't I count in this family? I have suffered every bit as much as my brother and I didn't do a damn thing to deserve it. Despite that, I've made something of myself. I have a nice, normal life with a husband, living in a house close enough that we can visit, and I even gave you a grandchild. Why don't I get anything for that? It's always poor Todd this and poor Todd that."

"Look, Lees, I get it," Faelan said, understanding her frustration. "You never had a fair shake because of me. But me staying here won't make things better, only worse."

She looked up at the ceiling, shaking her hands in frustration as she screamed, "I just want to be a normal family!"

Faelan put his arms around her and held his sister until she quieted. "Lees, I never told you this, but I admire what you've done, every part of it. Including that kid of yours in the other room. You are what keeps this family ticking. When I fuck up, at least I know Mom and Pop have you." He rubbed the top of her head like he used to when they were kids. "You're the bomb, fart-face."

She glared up at him, but slowly she cracked a smile. "Whatever, dickweed."

Their mother shook her head, never caring for their affectionate terms for one another.

Lisa pushed away from him, pointing at his face. "Don't think this gets you off the hook. You *are* going to be the best damn uncle in the world."

"Scouts honor," he replied, holding up his three fingers in salute, just like the old days.

"When are you leaving, son?" his father asked.

Faelan answered, not trying to sugarcoat it. "As soon as possible, Pop."

"Why so soon?" his mother cried out.

Lisa shook her head, growling. "So typical of my brother…" She stormed out of the room.

Faelan looked at his dad and shrugged apologetically.

His father replied, "A man's gotta do what a man's gotta do."

Faelan noticed his mother stand up, her eyes darting around the kitchen. He was certain she was mentally assessing the things she could load him up with before he left. There was a time when he would have resented it, but now he understood it was the way she coped. Giving him things was an expression of love, even if the items themselves were not wanted or needed.

"Hey, Mom, why don't you sit next to me," Faelan

said, patting the kitchen chair beside him.

Lisa came back into the room carrying the baby, who was still fussy. "If you're leaving, then you are holding Joshua until you leave. Get that uncle time in there, dickweed." She plopped her kid on his lap and moved over to the other side of the table to sit with her husband.

Faelan looked down at the unhappy little tyke and smiled mischievously. "Hey there, Joshua. Wanna know your mommy's real name?" He bent down, cupping the infant's ear and whispering.

Suddenly a plush toy bounced off his head.

"Don't be bad-mouthing me to my own son," Lisa warned.

Faelan looked up and shrugged. "I'm pretty sure that's what uncles do. Give their sisters a bad time and spoil the kid rotten with candy and loud toys." He gazed back down at Joshua and smiled. "Am I right, little guy?"

Lisa shook her head, but Faelan could tell things were okay between them. Even though he could never make up for what happened to her in the past, at least he could be there for her kid. Maybe, in some small way, that would make a difference.

Faelan was on a plane to LA the following week. As the large aircraft made a circle over the plains of Colorado before heading toward the mountains and California, he felt a surge of relief.

Tono Nosaka had encouraged him that he was meant for greater things, and for the first time he was finally starting to believe it. This second chance in LA might be the ticket to making a life of significance. Something to make up for Trevor's death, his sister's pain, and Nosaka's sacrifice.

Carrying the burden of so many debts was sobering, but something had fundamentally changed. He could feel it, like a shift in the Universe.

Rubbing his abdomen, he looked out the window as the Denver skyline disappeared in the distance. He was heading toward something. Good or bad—he was ready to attack it full force.

And the first thing he did after he landed was to sign up to do a session at the Haven. He'd missed the interaction with the subs and the banter back and forth with other Doms.

It had been some time since he'd frequented the place, so it was not too surprising people didn't recognize him at first. The clientele had changed after Brie's first documentary, becoming a mix of experienced kinksters and the curious. Still, it seemed to give the place an underlying energy that he could feed off of.

Faelan was pleased to see Captain with his arm wrapped around his tiny sub's waist approach him at the bar. Holding out a hand, the older man said, "I see the prodigal son has returned."

Faelan laughed as he shook his hand firmly. "I have."

Candy gave him a slight bow before gracing him with a warm smile. "Your presence has been missed, Mr. Wallace." She whispered to her Dom who nodded. With permission given, she gave Faelan a hug and told him, "I was afraid I would never see you again and I couldn't bear the thought of it."

He smiled as he patted the area of his healing incision. "It took the community, as well as the love and heartbreak of a good woman, but I'm finally back."

Candy cringed. "I was sorry to hear about Mary."

Faelan shook his head.

Okay, it still hurt. But this—right now—felt good.

"I apologize for saying anything," she immediately blurted, bowing as she stared hard at the ground.

"No, don't be," he replied. "You are invested in Mary's welfare. Just because we aren't together doesn't change your connection with her. I appreciate that you care."

"You both are in our thoughts," she said as she stepped back to rejoin her Master.

Faelan looked to Captain. "Have you seen her?"

He shook his head briskly once. "*Leif* is being evasive. I have no time for such games, but am keeping tabs on her."

"I'm glad." He frowned. "She needs your support, but she can be stubborn and spiteful when she gets in these moods."

Captain pressed his lips together in a thin line. "Yes. I don't want that to be her undoing."

"Me either," Faelan agreed.

"So, who's this handsome specimen?" asked a slicked-back, black-haired Dominatrix dressed in shiny latex as she slinked up beside him and looked Faelan over brazenly.

"Mistress Desire, this is Faelan. A graduate of the Dominant Training Center."

She smiled seductively. "A fellow graduate, huh? I'm surprised I don't know you."

"I've been on a sabbatical of sorts," Faelan replied, being equally brazen as he sized her up.

"And did you learn what you needed?" she asked, running her tongue against her bottom lip.

"I did, and then some." Faelan nodded to the manager of the club, who was letting him know the alcove was ready.

"Mr. Wallace, let me just say that I am thrilled you have returned. Many a sub has asked for you since you left, missing the spontaneous scenes you were known for. When I told them you were coming tonight, word spread quickly. I think you will find an ample selection to choose from."

"Thank you, Roger. I appreciate you fitting me in tonight with such short notice."

"My pleasure, Mr. Wallace." The manager gave him a slight head nod before leaving to attend to a disturbance on the other side of the room.

"Do you mind if I watch?" the Dominatrix asked as he bent down and grabbed his tool bag.

"Not at all," Faelan smiled. "I prefer to be watched."

He turned to Captain and Candy. "If you'll please excuse me."

Faelan left them with Mistress Desire following behind him. He was definitely back in the game, and felt good to be a wolf on the prowl.

He instructed the Mistress to stand back as he took

one of the papers from the box and began perusing the fantasies the subs had written. They were not allowed to include their names, which allowed him to choose the fantasy not the girl.

He liked the challenge and spontaneity of this setup. Not knowing beforehand how the night would play out or who he would be playing with kept him on his toes, and allowed him to practice a variety of tools continuously so he didn't lose his touch. It also made the subs at the Haven very happy.

The other Doms at the club enjoyed it as well because observing the wide variety of fantasies Faelan acted out gave them new fodder to use during their own private sessions.

Faelan considered the fantasies private property and never let anyone read them, always disposing of them personally when the night was through. A sexual fantasy was a unique window into a woman's soul, and not something to be shared, no matter how desperately the other Doms begged him.

After going through this night's selection, he picked the one he wanted to play out and slipped it in his pocket. He poured the others back into the box and placed it in his bag.

While he was setting up the simple scene, he spotted a short, curvy brunette hiding in the shadows, quietly observing him. Normally, he wouldn't have thought anything of it but there was something about her. The way she stared at him so intensely gave Faelan the impression she knew him even though he did not recognize her.

He pretended not to notice her, but hoped after the night was over he would be able to track her down and find out what, if any, their connection was.

As was tradition, when he was ready to announce the winning fantasy, Faelan hit a thick cane twice in quick succession against one of the metal support beams. The low, ringing sound it made traveled through the air, alerting everyone interested to come gather.

Once a sizable crowd had formed, he pulled the slip of paper out of his pocket and smiled at the group. "First, I want to thank you for welcoming me back into the Haven fold. It's nice to know that you can always come home."

After pausing for a moment for the enthusiastic applause of hopeful subs, he announced, "I've decided on my first night back that something unusual is in order. This particular fantasy reminds me of my training days as a Dominant and I am feeling in a particularly nostalgic mood tonight."

Unfolding the paper, he began reading.

Master Faelan, I have been a longtime fan of your work. I have followed you ever since Brie Bennett filmed the documentary about the Training Center and I heard her talk about her very first session with you. The fact you were able to win her over with such a simple tool speaks to your gift as a Dominant. I would like to taste that raw power with the very instrument you used during that first encounter. You have my permission to have your way with me.

He held up the paper and called out, "Who wrote this?"

A thin woman with long straight hair and big brown eyes of Indian descent moved forward as the other subs parted to make way for her.

Faelan held out his palm to the submissive and grasped her delicate hand in his. "And your name is?"

"*Viri*, Master Faelan."

He gave her a charming smile. "Call me Faelan. It is my formal title and encourages the primal animal in me."

She shuddered in delight, a wide smile spreading across her face. "Thank you, Faelan."

"Do you have an aversion to chains?"

She shook her head, her eyes growing wider.

"And when you stated I had permission to have my way with you?"

She bit her lip for a moment before answering. "I wish you to be intimate with me, if that is your pleasure."

He wrapped his arm around her waist and grinned wickedly as he guided her to the center of the alcove. "I am pleased to inform you that you will have the *entirety* of your fantasy played out."

She looked up at him in adoration before gazing back at the floor, her submissive posture inviting his play.

"Before we begin, however, I want you to undress completely and stand facing your audience."

Faelan observed her closely as she followed through with his orders. What *viri* lacked in practiced grace she made up for with enthusiasm. The radiant joy on her face told the world how she felt being his submissive for the scene.

Wanting to bring a more visually stimulating element to the original scene, Faelan cuffed her to the overhanging chains, letting the tantalizing sound of the clinking metal add to her excitement.

Pulling them taut to keep her stance long and lean, he circled around her, taking note of her small, pert breasts, her dark nipples erect with desire, and her smooth brown skin sprinkled with random beauty marks.

As he moved around her, he mentioned what he found appealing not only for her benefit, but for the crowd's.

"*Viri*, you have a stunning pussy, quite unusual..." He marveled at how the outer folds peeking from between her legs resembled delicate petals from a flower. A virtual flower for him to pluck.

Faelan lightly grazed the skin of her thigh as he moved behind her and admired her small, round ass. Every woman's body shape was different, and in the case of *viri*, her little ass reminded him of round melons on her skinny frame. Her buttocks were charming and begged to be squeezed.

He told her so as he completed his assessment before beginning the scene.

Turning to their audience, wanting to get them involved, he asked, "Does anyone know what the very first instrument I used happens to be?"

With the documentary having done so well in the LA market, he was not surprised when a multitude of hands went up.

Choosing the sub next to Mistress Desire, he said,

"Please enlighten everyone."

"A flogger?" she answered.

There were hushed groans as the other subs reacted to the incorrect answer, but they remained respectful, keeping the answer to themselves.

He shook his head at the sub who had answered, letting her know she was wrong. She looked at him sheepishly and promptly hid behind the Dominatrix.

"What is it?" one of the Dominants asked, obviously curious to find out what he was going to use on the sub bound so alluringly for rough play.

Rather than answer him, Faelan walked to his bag and pulled out a long flat box. He was purposely slow as he lifted the lid and took out a large white feather.

He heard chuckles from the crowd as the other Dominants dismissed the simple tool.

Faelan grinned inwardly as he took off his shirt, knowing he was about to school a bunch of cocky Doms.

Walking over to *viri*, he leaned down to hover next to her ear and whispered, "Stare straight ahead, *viri*. Let those in attendance read your face as we play."

She nodded, goosebumps forming on her skin in anticipation of his touch. There was something to be said about playing with groupies. The amount of expectancy built up in their minds meant little effort was needed on his end. In a case like this, he would be able to milk it for an extended period and help this girl achieve orgasm multiple times.

Faelan moved in close behind her so she could feel the strength of his body next to hers, but not quite touch. With his physical dominance stated, he let the light touch of the feather do its erotic work as he glided it over her.

Viri whimpered in pleasure.

Faelan looked up from her shoulder at the Dom who asked which instrument he'd used. With a wicked smile, he trailed the feather over *viri's* breasts and then slowly glided it down her stomach to her mound. His eyes still on the Dom, Faelan growled in her ear as the feather tickled her pussy, and left the lightest of bites on her shoulder as it grazed her clit.

Viri trembled where she stood, making the chains rattle above her as she orgasmed in front of the crowd.

Faelan glanced over at Mistress Desire knowingly, and was gratified to see her smirk as she silently made a clapping motion.

Yes, he knew how to tease and satisfy both his sub and the audience simultaneously. He considered it his special gift.

Now that he had decided to call California his home, Faelan decided to take a path similar to the one Thane Davis had taken as Headmaster of the Training Center. He would keep his emotions out of the exchanges.

After his failed relationship with Mary, he had no stomach for love or the complications it invited. Being a man of extreme passions, he loved too openly and too fiercely.

Loyal to a fault, he had breathed and lived for his woman to the point that he'd become utterly lost in her. Now that it was over with Mary, he realized his heart couldn't survive that level of pain again.

Even though Brie had brought meaning into his life and Mary had brought a greater understanding—and he did not regret either relationship—he knew he could not survive another heartbreak.

It was better for everyone if he kept an emotional distance and focused on improving his skills while entertaining the masses. It's where his real satisfaction came from. Who knew, maybe he would become a trainer at the Center and truly follow in Davis's footsteps.

That would be a humorous turn of events.

As Faelan was plowing his cock into *viri* at the end of their session, after wringing numerous orgasms from the girl, he noticed the woman in the shadows watching him again.

He had to look away from her or risk losing his rhythm. Gripping *viri* tight, he gave her what her wet pussy had been begging for the last hour—a deep, satisfying pounding as he came inside her.

Her sweet cries of passion rang through the club as she came a final time.

The rattling of the chains came to an end as he released her from the cuffs and escorted her to the corner of the alcove. He held *viri* close to him, stroking her hair and talking to her in a low, calming tone.

When he glanced up, he saw the mystery girl disappearing into the crowd. He wanted to chase her down, but his duty was to the sub he'd just played with. Curbing his curiosity, Faelan returned his attention to the girl in his arms.

All in all, it had been a triumphant return.

Rytsar's Enlistment

Faelan answered the doorbell for Marquis and saw the surprised look on Rytsar Durov's face as he stood at the doorstep.

The Russian frowned. "What are you doing here?"

"Didn't you know? I live here now," he said with amusement.

Durov grunted his displeasure but entered the house, brushing past him. "Living with the parents. Fitting, I guess," he replied dismissively as he made his way down the hallway.

Faelan smiled to himself as he followed the man, finding the Russian's early morning rudeness entertaining. He did not engage him further, however, because Marquis had warned him that the man was here on serious business.

"Mr. Durov, what an honor to have you join us this morning," Celestia said in greeting, giving a quick bow as he passed.

Faelan would have retreated to his room, but Marquis called out to him. "Please join us." While Marquis and Durov took a seat in the study, Faelan chose to stand—suddenly feeling on edge.

"I did not expect the boy to be here," Rytsar complained. "The news is not meant for his ears."

Marquis looked at Faelan with confidence. "I want you to know that Mr. Wallace is someone I have come to admire and trust."

Faelan was humbled by Marquis's words, but Durov was not impressed and glared at him in distrust.

"You know how I feel about you."

Faelan raised an eyebrow. "The feeling's mutual, I assure you. However, Marquis mentioned that Brie is somehow involved and needs help."

"Why would I let you have anything to do with Mrs. Davis, after the shit you pulled on them after the collaring?" he scoffed.

"I have matured since then. Thane, Brie, and I have made our peace."

Durov looked back at Marquis. "Would you trust this man with Brie's life?"

Marquis didn't hesitate. "Yes."

The Russian looked back at Faelan, sizing him up. "If Thane wasn't conscious, I wouldn't even consider it. But now, if you make a misstep, you will have to answer to him."

"Did you say Mr. Davis is conscious?" Marquis questioned.

Faelan felt a surge of relief hearing that he was recovering from the plane crash. "I knew he would fight his way back. He's an even tougher bastard than I am."

"And you remember that, Wolfpup," Durov warned,

pointing at him.

Marquis directed them back to the reason for Durov's visit. "You do not appear to have time to waste if I'm reading you correctly."

"True." Durov motioned Faelan to sit, physically including him in the discussion. "I'll make this quick and to the point. Thane's half-sister plotted to kill Brie's baby and send Brie off into slavery. She came dangerously close, but Nosaka prevented the kidnapping."

Both Marquis and Faelan were shocked by the revelation.

"What the hell? You can't be serious," Faelan exclaimed.

Marquis's voice remained calm. "Lilly is behind bars now, I assume."

"No!" Rytsar shouted angrily, as if it were his fault. "Your American authorities were unable to catch her and the threat being too great for Brie, I took it upon myself to handle the situation. With a little time and persuasion, she finally confessed to her crimes."

Marquis stiffened. "Are you saying you kidnapped and tortured Thane's sister?"

"Half-sister, and no. I merely detained her and manipulated her living conditions. Because she carries a child, I was extremely careful not to cause harm to the baby." He looked at Faelan. "The woman is deranged. She has been blackmailing Thane since China, claiming the child she carried was his even though it is another man's child."

"You have got to be fucking kidding me," Faelan growled.

"I assure you I'm not. Her level of madness goes even deeper. She is in love with him and hoped to become intimate partners."

Marquis's expression became more somber as he listened to Rytsar, but he was resolute. "This woman should be in the hospital, not under your *care*."

Faelan could see that Marquis's statement vexed Durov, and for once he was on the Russian's side.

"You do not appreciate the grave threat she poses to Brie," Rytsar insisted. "If the authorities were unable to arrest her, what makes you think a psych ward would be able to keep her from escaping?" he asked, adding, "I guarantee she will harm Brie if she escapes, and will remain a threat until her dying breath."

Marquis sat back for a moment, taking in what had been shared.

But the path was much clearer for Faelan and he asked, "What is it you want us to do?"

"I may have to leave suddenly in the next day or two, but I must be assured the threat will remain contained."

"I will not participate in a kidnapping," Marquis replied. "Whatever we do must be done legally and through proper channels."

"What are you suggesting?" Durov asked, trying to keep his irritation in check.

"Despite what you think, I do understand the danger she poses to both Brie and Sir Davis," Marquis assured him. "Therefore, we must 'arrange' for the police to find and arrest her, and it must be in a neutral area so you are not connected in any way."

The Russian chewed on the suggestion for several

moments before asking, "What if she escapes?"

Faelan felt as if everything had come into focus. This was the role he was destined to fill; already a solution was playing in his mind. Without hesitation he vowed, "I will do whatever it takes to protect Brie."

"Anything?" Durov pressed.

"As far as I am concerned, I owe Brie and Thane for every breath I take."

Durov stared hard at him. "You have to swear on your life that Lilly will not escape."

"I swear."

Marquis was more cautious in his reply. "I promise I will do everything in my power to keep this woman behind bars—not only for Brie's sake, but for her own."

While Durov accepted Marquis's stance, he turned back to Faelan and said in earnest, "I'm depending on you to fill in when the judicial system fails her."

"I will be ready," Faelan assured him. "I am not afraid to get my hands dirty."

The very next day Faelan looked down at his phone, surprised to see the Russian word **daleko** flash on the screen. Durov had informed him it meant "far, far away" and was the code word he would use if shit hit the fan.

This was much sooner than expected, but Faelan had spent the night discussing with Marquis in detail what they would do so he immediately put their plan into action.

Grabbing his car keys, he met with Marquis before heading out. After a quick glance at the address Durov had written, he nodded.

Marquis struck a match and lit the paper, throwing it into the fireplace to destroy any link to them. "I am curious why this is happening sooner than anticipated," he said as they both watched the flames take hold and the small piece of paper burned to ash.

"Something bad must have happened. There was no reason for him to rush this," Faelan stated, his heart rate increasing as he considered what lay ahead for them.

"It will all go as planned regardless," Marquis replied, unflustered by the unexpected turn of events.

"I'm headed out to verify the package makes it to the proper authorities. Otherwise, we will be facing a far bigger problem."

"Good. I will proceed to the payphone and report the location to the authorities just as we discussed with Durov." Marquis picked up a rag and stuffed it in his pocket. Faelan assumed it would be used to wipe off his prints once the call was made.

Marquis looked at Faelan and warned, "We must be thorough. Neither of us can afford to be implicated if things go awry."

Faelan grasped Marquis's arm. "If, for any reason, something goes wrong I will be the one to take the fall for this."

"It's not—"

Faelan shook his head, stating in a hushed voice, "You have Celestia and the Training Center's reputation to worry about. I refuse to put either in jeopardy."

Before Marquis could argue the point, Faelan headed out the door. He understood what was at stake. He had vowed to protect Brie and was determined to protect Marquis and Celestia in the process.

This decision was easy for him. Here was a concrete way to make up for all the harm he'd caused in the past. The fact it might require sacrifice made him that much more determined. These people had become as dear as his own family and he would not let them down, no matter the cost.

Faelan shook his head as he drove away from the house. Not once had Marquis ever called him Wolfpup, even though Faelan had acted immaturely on more than a few occasions, and he deeply respected Marquis for that.

The man was uncommonly wise—to the point he did not quite seem part of this world. And yet, Marquis related to all manner of people as long as they could accept his intensity and directness.

To be associated with Marquis Gray, much less invited into his private life, was a true honor no one else had been afforded. Faelan understood the privilege he'd been given.

He drove directly to the address Rytsar had written. The apartment building looked old, a humorous nod to the unusual architecture of the 60s, but Faelan spotted no police cars parked outside yet.

It made him anxious, but he remained where he was, trusting Marquis had already placed the anonymous call, and the police were not far away. It would be folly to risk being seen, so Faelan fought the urge to enter the apartment building himself.

Instead, he pulled out his phone and started scrolling through the newsfeed to keep himself from worrying. He stopped suddenly when he spotted raw black and white camera footage of Rytsar's violent takedown at the hospital.

"Oh shit…"

Faelan could see the outline of Brie cowering as Rytsar was beaten unconscious next to her. The hairs on the back of his neck rose as he watched them drag the Russian's limp body out of the room, all the while threating the staff with guns.

Now he was worried for Durov's life as well. Although he'd known the Russian was facing a bad situation, he never suspected it was as terrible as this.

Faelan was about to turn the volume up on his phone to learn more when he saw a police car pull up to the building. Slumping low in his seat to avoid being seen, Faelan watched as the two officers entered the apartment building quietly.

Keeping his eyes on the fourth-story window, Faelan watched just in case Lilly tried to make an escape.

The loud wail of a siren behind him made Faelan nearly jump as another police car pulled up to the front of the building behind the first one. Keeping himself hidden, Faelan watched as a bald, and very pregnant, woman was dragged out of the apartment building and "helped" into the backseat of the first car.

He could hear her screaming at the men as she struggled in her cuffs.

Faelan smiled to himself, appreciating Rytsar's creativity in using such a harmless tactic as shaving Lilly's head to humiliate her. He was determined to be equally resourceful.

Keeping his distance, Faelan followed behind the cops as they drove to the police station. He wanted to see that she physically made it inside the building before he left.

Faelan was taking no chances, having been warned by Durov about how conniving she was. Once she was escorted in handcuffs into the station, he called Brie, wanting to report to her directly about Lilly's incarceration, and to make sure Brie was all right after what had just happened.

It took several tries before she finally picked up.

"Hello?" she answered, her voice shaking.

"Hey, Brie. I just saw what happened to Durov on the news." He paused for a moment, knowing discretion was vital. "There is something I must to talk to you about, but not over the phone. Is it okay if I come there to meet you?"

"Mr. Wallace, thank you for your concern, but Sir and I are fine," she answered unconvincingly, then added, "and we're not up for visitors…"

It was obvious Durov hadn't had a chance to inform her of his involvement with Lilly. Certain that she would want to know, he headed to the hospital anyway. He texted Marquis to inform him where he was headed, certain Marquis would deduce the reason without explanation.

Faelan avoided the crowd of reporters at the entrance of the hospital by heading to the employee entrance through the back. He was able to sneak into Davis's room when a reporter made a ruckus trying to push his way through the staff of orderlies at the nurses' station.

Upon entering the room Faelan stopped short, unprepared for what he saw.

It was jarring to see how just how thin and gaunt Thane Davis was after being months in a coma. Brie was beside him by the bed, holding his hand and crying softly.

While Davis appeared diminished physically, the power of his presence was unmistakable. When Thane's gaze landed on Faelan, he fell momentarily mute.

"I…I'm sorry to disturb you both."

Brie looked up and protested in a weak voice, "But I told you not to come."

"I know," Faelan acknowledged, but he looked at Davis. "I'm here to speak to you on the orders of a mutual friend."

Davis narrowed his eyes and said in a gruff voice, "Come…closer."

Faelan moved beside Brie and spoke in a low tone, "I have news about Lilly."

Brie's face went white.

The nurse walked in and saw Brie's shocked face, so she immediately called for the orderlies to come.

"No," Brie told her, wiping her remaining tears away. "This is our friend, Todd Wallace. Please let him stay, and would you shut the door behind you?"

The nurse nodded, quickly exiting the room to explain to the orderlies that she'd made a mistake.

Once the door was closed, Davis turned his attention on Faelan. "Go on."

Not wanting to expose Marquis's involvement, Faelan explained, "Durov spoke with me yesterday. Together we formulated a plan to get Lilly behind bars as quickly as possible."

Brie broke into fresh tears.

"I want you both to know she has been arrested. I made sure personally so you can rest assured she is not a threat to you. I will continue to monitor the situation with her to guarantee it remains that way."

"You should not—" Sir began.

Faelan interrupted. "Durov asked me to manage the situation and that is what I intend to do without fail."

Brie's voice broke between sobs. "You…saw him…yesterday?"

"Yes, Brie. When he filled me in about what had happened with Lilly, I vowed I would protect you."

Brie whimpered, "He knew this was coming?"

Sir held out a shaking hand to touch Brie. She instantly quieted at her Master's touch, but the tears still fell silently as she looked up at Faelan.

"Although he mentioned his time was short, none of us were prepared for this."

Davis picked up on his choice of words and instantly questioned, "Who else?"

Faelan was instantly reminded just how astute Sir was. Being careful in his answer, he explained only part of the truth. "Durov's men were ordered to scatter. He was concerned about their safety."

Davis nodded. "The Koslov brothers are dangerous."

"As is Lilly," Faelan countered.

He noticed again how pale Brie became at the mention of the woman's name. "I promise I will not let her harm you."

Brie nodded, wrapping both her hands around her husband's hand for comfort.

"Thank you," Davis stated hoarsely.

Faelan explained, "I'm here for you both in whatever capacity you need. I owe you for my life."

Davis shook his head. "You owe nothing."

Faelan snorted in disagreement. "You found my donor on the other side of the world when I'd all but given up." Faelan looked down at Brie kindly. "And you cared for me when I was being a total jerk in the hospital—even making sure I had chocolate and dubstep."

Brie's sad eyes softened.

Faelan confessed to Davis, "I remember when you told me 'There are families formed by blood and others by character.'"

Davis nodded slowly.

"Well, you guys, and that crazy Russian, are now part of my family." Faelan smirked, adding, "Whether you like it or not."

Brie lowered her head and let out a sob.

Faelan looked to Davis apologetically, realizing Durov was a touchy subject for her.

"Tell us what…you know," Sir rasped, petting Brie's hair gently.

Faelan pulled up a chair beside the bed, keeping his voice low and his eyes on the door as he shared what had transpired with Lilly. He knew any overheard mention of her name could put everyone he cared about in jeopardy.

"Do you know where they took Rytsar?" Brie asked desperately, when he told them about his meeting with the man.

"I only know he said his time was short, Brie. He didn't go into detail why."

Brie buried her head in her hands.

Davis looked at him sadly. "We are both…still in shock."

"Is there anything I can do to h—"

The door swung wide as Anderson walked in with the nurse behind him.

"I hope this is okay," she apologized. "He wouldn't take no for an answer."

Anderson broke into a wide smile. "It's a damn welcomed sight to see those eyes open, buddy."

Brie looked up and smiled through her tears. "Master Anderson." She got up and walked over to him, laying her head against his chest.

Anderson looked at Davis somberly as he wrapped his arms around her in a bear hug.

Faelan watched Davis rather than the interaction between Brie and Anderson. The man had a slight smile on his face, obviously pleased his old friend had arrived.

Master Anderson lifted Brie off the floor and walked her back over to Davis. "I came as soon as I saw it on the news."

Davis shook his head. "I wish there wasn't…a video of it."

Master Anderson set Brie down, nodding in understanding.

"It hurts to watch it," Brie whimpered, the tears starting up again.

"Young Brie, you know how I am with tears," Master Anderson chided warmly. Faelan understood he was trying to get her to smile, but it backfired and she looked over at Faelan, her chin trembling as she tried to hold it in.

"You can cry on me," Faelan answered, patting his shirt.

She smiled slightly—a small victory.

Master Anderson turned to face Faelan, frowning. "Explain to me exactly why *you* are here."

Davis lifted his hand up, the muscles of his arm shaking from the effort. "He's helpin—"

When he started coughing, Brie grabbed a cup of water from the bed tray and tipped the cup to help him drink as she said gently, "No more talking, Sir."

Brie told both men, "We have to keep our questions to a simple yes or no."

Anderson nodded, glancing at Faelan with nervous concern when the nurse rushed in to check on Davis.

It was easy to see in the expression on Anderson's face that the man was deeply worried about his friend. Because Faelan knew all too well how difficult recovery was, he wasn't nearly as concerned.

After the nurse left, being satisfied with his vitals, Faelan asked Davis, "Do you know where they took him?"

Davis shook his head.

"Is there someone you need us to contact?"

He nodded.

Faelan turned to Brie. "Do you know the name?"

"No," she answered, looking bereft.

"How about you?" he asked Anderson.

"I'd suggest Titov. That's Rytsar's right-hand man." Anderson looked at Davis. "Is that who you are suggesting we call first?"

Davis nodded again.

"I have his number," Brie offered, fishing her phone out of her purse. Her hand was still shaking as she handed it to Anderson.

Faelan stopped him, stating, "I think I should be the one to call."

"Why? Rytsar's been my friend since college."

"He came to me yesterday to ask for my assistance."

Anderson furrowed his brow and turned to Davis. "Why the hell would he go to Wolfpup?"

Faelan bristled at the nickname but remained silent.

Davis looked equally surprised and looked to Faelan for the answer.

Still mindful of protecting Marquis and Celestia, Faelan told them, "It wasn't as if I was his first choice, by any means. But Durov found himself in a tight spot and suspected he didn't have any time. I vowed not to let Thane or Brie down."

"This doesn't feel right," Anderson complained.

"He knows about…" Brie whispered the name, "…Lilly," to Anderson, adding, "Rytsar wouldn't have told him about her if he didn't trust him."

Anderson eyed Faelan suspiciously. "You know what happened to her?"

Faelan nodded.

"Where is she now?" he demanded.

"In jail."

"How do you know this?"

Faelan pulled out his phone and showed a picture he'd taken of Lilly being escorted into the police station.

"That doesn't look like her," Anderson scoffed.

"It is," Davis insisted.

Anderson shook his head, growling. "I would do anything for you both. I don't understand why I was kept out of the loop here." He closed his eyes for a moment and then sighed in frustration, muttering, "That sadistic bastard…"

Faelan had no idea who he was talking about, until Brie said to Anderson. "I'm sure it wasn't personal. Todd said himself that Rytsar was out of time, and…" Her eyes started to well up with tears. "He…was. You don't know this, but someone tried to kill him yesterday. He barely escaped."

"What are you talking about?" Faelan asked, this being the first he'd heard of it.

"An assassin tried take him out, but Shadow saved him."

"That damn cat?" Anderson asked in disbelief.

Brie nodded sadly, then looked at Faelan. "Master Gannon's cat."

"From the Sanctuary?"

"Yes."

Faelan's head was swimming with all this new information.

"Did you know that Master Gannon had passed?"

"Yes, it was hard news to hear. He was an exceptional man." Faelan glanced away from her, feeling the pain of that loss again. "Gannon was good to both Mary and me."

Brie nodded her agreement.

As far as Faelan knew, Brie was unaware of their breakup and he wasn't about to tell her under the circumstances, so he swallowed the pain but couldn't hide it.

The sympathetic look on Master Anderson's face alerted Faelan to the fact he'd heard the news about Mary. Probably through Lea, Faelan guessed.

As a gesture of solidarity, Master Anderson threw out something to defuse the situation. "Young Brie, I've been meaning to talk to you about your little cat story…"

She blushed, a smile returning to her wet cheeks. "Did you like it?"

"Before I answer I have to know, did Durov put you up to it?"

"Oh no, I wrote the story myself. Call it…an inspiration of sorts. But when I was finished I read it to both Rytsar and Sir." She looked at her Master lovingly. "That's when Rytsar suggested I send it, along with the card." She smiled back at Anderson. "He said it would cheer you up."

"Of course he did…"

Brie looked at him with concern. "Wait. So you *didn't* like the story?"

Rubbing his chin, Anderson said, "Let's just say I found it highly unusual and a tad disturbing."

"But I honestly believe Cayenne and Shadow have a

special bond, Master Anderson," she insisted. "I only meant to express my joy for Cayenne's motherhood and to assure you of Shadow's romantic intentions."

He shook his head. "You still insist on that, knowing how it was for her?"

"Pain can be sexy, you know." Brie grinned, her tears momentarily forgotten. "Aren't you living proof of that?"

Master Anderson smirked. "Touché."

"What the heck are you talking about?" Faelan asked, amused by the odd banter.

"Wondering as well," Davis stated.

Brie turned to Sir with a look of compassion. "I read it to you, but I'm not surprised you don't remember. It makes me wonder how much you don't remember…"

"My memories are…a jumbled mess."

Brie leaned over and kissed him on the lips. "We'll unravel that together, Sir." She lay her head on his chest and looked at Faelan and Anderson.

What she had been through, what was still ahead for them both, made his troubles seem inconsequential. Faelan glanced at Anderson with a half-smile and gave him a slight nod, grateful for the man's sensitivity and help.

"Call Titov now," Davis commanded.

Faelan took Brie's phone from her and dialed the number. It rang only once before the recording stated, "This number has been disconnected…"

"It's no longer working," he informed them.

Davis frowned, letting out a long sigh.

"What does it mean?" Master Anderson asked Faelan.

"They are all…in danger," Davis answered, closing his eyes, his brow furrowed in concern.

"All of them?" Brie cried softly.

Davis nodded, stating without opening his eyes, "The Koslovs are ruthless."

Brie looked at Faelan with desperation. "Do you have any other way to reach him—anybody?"

He shook his head. "No, Durov only told me what I needed to do. There was no backup plan."

"Damn…" Anderson muttered. "But they all can't vanish into thin air."

"They must to survive," Davis answered hoarsely.

"What do we do now?" Anderson asked.

Davis braced his arms on the bed rails and slowly forced his body to sit more upright. "First, I have to get out of this damn bed." He started coughing again from the strain.

Brie gave both men an exasperated look as if it were their fault, before grabbing the glass of water and coaxing him to drink it.

The nurse came back in. "Do they need to leave?" she asked Davis.

"No," he answered, followed by another round of coughing.

The nurse turned to Brie for an answer.

She shook her head. "It's not them, it's him," she said, pointing to her Master. "He's pushing himself too hard."

"I have to get out of bed," he growled, looking at the nurse for understanding.

"That's going to take some time," she told him, "but you'll get there."

"I don't have time."

The nurse looked at him apologetically.

Davis glanced at Faelan, the pain in his eyes hard to bear. "He cannot die."

"We won't let that happen," Anderson assured him.

He put his hand on Faelan's shoulder, and Faelan agreed, "We've got your back."

"Would you like me to get you a sedative?" the nurse asked. "The doctor recommended it, and rest is important for your recovery."

Davis glared at her.

Brie moved between them, assuring the nurse as she quickly escorted her out of the room, "He promises to rest."

When she was gone, Brie returned to her Master and asked, "Sir, what can Faelan and Master Anderson do to help Rytsar?"

Faelan felt the buzz of his phone and looked down to see a new text from Celestia.

A package just arrived addressed to you w/ no return address.

Faelan immediately told Davis, "I may have something here. Give me a minute."

He texted back, asking Celestia to give the package to Marquis. It was vital to keep her as far away from this as possible.

A few minutes later, he got a text from Marquis.

You have received several items.

Faelan understood he was being purposely vague and replied similarly.

Worth returning home for?

The answer was simple and direct.

Yes

He looked up at Davis. "I'm headed out. I may have something that could shed some light."

"You need me to come with you?" Anderson asked.

"No, stay here with Davis. I'll return if it turns out to be useful."

Faelan shook Davis's hand before leaving the room. As he was walking down the hall, he heard Brie's voice calling behind him.

"Todd! Todd Wallace!"

He stopped, waiting for her to catch up. "You know the longer you keep me here, the more time we waste."

"I'm going with you."

He looked at her in surprise. "It's better if you didn't."

"Sir insisted."

Faelan glanced at the door of his room, wondering what Davis was thinking. Like Marquis with Celestia, his desire was to keep Brie as uninvolved as possible. "I don't think it's wise."

"Well, Sir does, and I'm not questioning it."

Faelan growled in frustration. "For the record I think

this is a bad idea."

Brie nodded and pressed the elevator button, asking, "Where's your car parked?"

Faelan had to trust Davis knew what he was doing as he escorted Brie to his 'stang and sped off.

Meeting with Marquis

Brie glanced at him several times while they drove before saying in a hushed voice, "It was so terrible…"

Faelan understood she'd remained strong for her Master, even though she was shattered by Durov's attack. "I couldn't believe the footage."

"He was so calm…" Her voice was tainted with anguish. "He met them straight on without any thought to himself."

Faelan reached out to her. "It was obvious yesterday how much he cares about you and Thane."

She looked straight ahead and murmured, "He might be dead…"

Faelan squeezed her arm before putting his hand back on the wheel, a natural habit for him because of the accident—*both hands on the wheel at all times.* "You can't think like that, Brie."

"He was prepared to die, Faelan. I've never seen him like that. It scares me now."

He understood her slipup in his title had everything

to do with her current state of distress and chose not to mention it to her, even though he preferred being called by that title. Surnames provided an emotional distance, which had purpose, but there were times, like this, when protocol had to take a backseat.

"Brie, we proceed from here believing he is alive. To think otherwise will waste precious energy and may cause his demise."

Brie closed her eyes, tears rolling down her cheeks.

"I know you're worried, and you've had to be strong this whole time."

"I'm panicking, Faelan," she stated, her eyes focused straight ahead.

Brie was teetering on a dangerous emotional cliff. Faelan suddenly realized that might have been the reason Davis sent her along. He understood Brie needed to either release it or she would be consumed by it.

Faelan felt extremely protective seeing her in this vulnerable state. He would do anything to protect her—from Lilly, from the Koslov brothers, and even herself, if necessary.

"Since you are coming with me, I must warn you that Celestia has no idea what is going on, and Marquis and I want to keep it that way. Nothing you hear or see can be shared with her."

"Marquis knows?"

Faelan gave her a rueful smile. "Marquis was Durov's first choice. I was an unwanted addition because I was there when Durov came to him for help." Faelan turned his head toward her briefly. "But I am a better fit for this job, Brie. Even Durov realized that once we talked.

Besides, the last thing either Marquis or Celestia need is to get entangled in this mess."

Brie shook her head. With too much information being thrown at her all at once, she could not process. Wanting to reassure her, he said, "Just so you and I are straight on this point. My first priority is to protect you from Lilly. Everything I do will be filtered through that objective."

He looked back at the road, hoping that knowledge would give her some comfort as she tried to take it all in.

Eventually, he felt the soft touch of Brie's hand on his shoulder. "I'm sorry you had to get involved."

"I'm not."

He hit his blinker and pulled to the side of the road and turned the car off so that he could give her his full attention. "I appreciate this opportunity to help you and Thane. You gave me my life back, even if you didn't know it at the time. So whatever happens, I have no regrets. I owe you both."

"You don't owe me anything, Faelan," she said, her sincerity tugging at his heart.

"Let me put it another way then. Ever since the accident back in high school, I have lived with the guilt of Trevor's death. Helping you is an extension of the payment I owe him for surviving."

"You almost died yourself in that accident. You don't owe anyone," she asserted.

He gave her a faint smile. "Then let's just say I want to do this—for myself." He started the engine back up and peeled out, knowing there was no more time to waste.

Faelan didn't bother knocking when he entered Marquis's house. When Celestia saw Brie she cried out in joy.

"Oh my goodness. What a blessed surprise!"

It was obvious by her cheerful reaction that she had not seen the news and had no idea of Durov's situation.

Thankfully, Brie was aware enough to pick up on that fact and smiled kindly at her. "So you must have heard that Sir has awakened?"

"Oh yes! We were so thrilled to hear the good news when the distinguished Rytsar Durov graced us with a visit yesterday. Did he give Sir Davis the gift I sent?"

Brie faltered for a moment upon hearing Durov's name. "No…I—"

"I'm sure in all the excitement he must have forgotten. Totally understandable," Celestia gushed.

"Is that Mrs. Davis I hear?" Marquis called out, coming from down the hallway.

It only took one look at Marquis before Brie burst into tears.

Marquis wrapped his arms around her. "There, there… I'm sure all of this is overwhelming. Why don't you join me in the study?"

He then turned his attention on Celestia. "Make us some tea and your famous lemon cookies, my love."

Celestia's face lit up. "It would be my greatest pleasure, Master."

Faelan followed Marquis and Brie into the study and shut the double doors behind him.

"What do you have for me?" Faelan asked.

Marquis opened his desk drawer and pulled out a large envelope. "He was thorough, even in the short time he had." He handed it over to Faelan and gestured for Brie to sit before he took a seat himself.

Faelan pulled out the contents to look them over. He frowned as he read Rytsar's hastily written note.

Mr. Wallace,

You have access to one of my accounts. Take what you need to guarantee Brie's safety. You will find that money acts as an excellent lubricant.

Due diligence is what I expect. Whatever it takes by any means necessary.

I am including a list of local contacts. I suggest you hire the first two on the list for surveillance purposes, but there are several who specialize in unique skills you may have use for later. I leave such decisions to your discretion.

Above all else—do not fail her.

~Rytsar

Faelan looked over the bank account information and the list Rytsar had provided with an overwhelming sense of relief. The Russian had left him with the means to ensure Lilly remained a nonthreat.

He looked up from the papers and told Marquis, "I will make good use of this."

"I don't want to know the details."

"Of course not." As he folded up the note, he glanced over at Brie.

"Is it from Rytsar?" she asked in the barest whisper.

"It is."

"May I read it?"

Brie's eyes were focused on the piece of paper in his hand as if it were a life preserver and she was drowning in an ocean.

Faelan looked to Marquis, who shook his head slowly.

"It is not meant for you," Faelan explained to Brie.

"I understand, but I need to read it. Please," she begged, her eyes expressing the desperation in her voice.

Looking over the note again, Faelan decided not to keep it from her, despite Marquis's reservations. He believed it might bring Brie a sense of security knowing there would be others ensuring her safety.

Handing the folded paper to her, Faelan said somberly, "This must stay between us."

Brie hesitated for a moment before nodding and taking it. She opened the note, the paper shaking in her hands as she read its contents.

Suddenly she burst into tears, clutching the paper against her chest.

Marquis stood up and offered her a handkerchief, shooting a disapproving look at Faelan.

Brie dabbed her eyes, letting out an anguished sob. "Up to the end, he was thinking of me…"

Marquis placed his hand on her shoulder, advising in a calm voice, "Work within the parameters that Durov will escape his captors."

Brie swallowed down the next sob and nodded. It seemed his authoritative tone brought her reassurance.

Although Marquis believed it had been a mistake to share it, Faelan had no regrets.

There were times, when the heart was involved, that you had to throw caution to the wind.

Brie stood up and turned to face Faelan, her eyes red from the many tears. "Thank you for sharing his note. It helps even though it hurts."

He took the note from her hand, smiling. "Anytime, blossom."

The slight upturn of her lips let him know she appreciated his attempt to keep it light. Taking a deep breath, Brie thoroughly dried her tears before handing the handkerchief back to Marquis.

"Mrs. Davis," Marquis explained, "I wish to keep Celestia away from anything to do with the *bratva* or Thane's half-sister. The less said in her presence, the better."

Brie frowned. "I wish none of you had to be involved."

"Not to worry," he assured her. "At this point the situation with Lilly has been dealt with, so now we can turn our focus to Durov."

"Lilly cannot be counted out," Faelan cautioned.

Marquis shook his head. "I know Durov insisted she remains dangerous, but I believe the woman is mentally unstable and will now get the medical help she sorely needs."

Brie stared at Marquis in disbelief. "I do *not* feel safe just because she's in jail. You don't know how cunning and cruel she is."

"That goes along with what Durov said, but I'm sure you agree the woman is mentally ill and needs care."

Brie grasped her belly protectively. "The only thing I

know is that she tried to kill my baby! I have zero compassion for her. None."

Marquis met her gaze. "You have every right to feel that way, Mrs. Davis."

"Although she is behind bars, my vigilance will not falter," Faelan vowed. "I have no illusions about the effectiveness of our penal system. Violent criminals get released all the time."

"She will look for a way out—legally or otherwise," Brie stated with certainty.

Faelan put his hands on her shoulders, looking directly into her eyes so she would be left with no doubts. "I am preparing for when she does."

Brie nodded and mouthed the words, "Thank you."

Sliding Rytsar's note back into the envelope, Faelan told Marquis, "I'll need to take care of this."

"Agreed. You should go, and I will take care of Mrs. Davis while you're out."

"No, we talked about this," Faelan insisted.

"While I appreciate the sentiment, Mr. Wallace, now that Durov has been taken, Sir Davis will insist on getting involved. Brie can return with me to the hospital so I can speak with him personally while you run your errands."

"This is not what you and I discussed. You are not supposed to get involved."

"Durov's capture changes our previous arrangement."

Faelan shook his head, frowning in disapproval. "I told you. I'm willing to get as dirty as I need to—on both counts. There's no reason both of us need to get involved."

"But you are wrong."

"How so?" Faelan demanded.

"We will have to gather all of our resources to have any chance of rescu—"

There was a light knock on the door.

Marquis gave both Brie and Faelan a look of warning before stating lightly, "Come in, Celestia."

His sub walked in holding a plate of freshly baked cookies, the aroma of which proceeded her. She smiled at her Master as she placed it on the coffee table.

"I thought you and our guests could enjoy these while I get your tea, Master." She turned around with a twinkle in her eye, shutting the doors behind her.

The citrus scent of lemons wafted through the air, causing Faelan's stomach to growl.

Marquis nodded toward the plate. "Please, take as many as you like. I find citrus clears the mind and makes it easier to think."

Faelan grabbed one of the cookies, handing it to Brie before taking three more for himself.

When he noticed Marquis watching him, he asked, "What? Aren't you having any?"

"I'm not hungry."

Faelan grabbed one off the plate and tossed it at him. "Too bad, we all need to think clearly right now."

Marquis deftly caught the cookie and chuckled amiably. "True enough."

Celestia returned with a large tray and set it down gracefully. With practiced precision, she poured each cup, handing the first to her Master. She then gave the next to Faelan, and to the last cup she added a small decoration before handing it to Brie.

It was a single dandelion flower, its stem weaved around the handle of the cup.

She smiled at Brie as she offered it. "I saw it outside the kitchen window and thought of you—so joyful and resilient."

Brie stared at the bright yellow flower. "I've never thought of dandelions that way before, but I like the comparison. Thank you."

"Dandelions are one of my favorites, just ask my Master."

Marquis smiled at Celestia with amusement. "I can attest to her love of the weed."

"It's only a weed because a man gave it that classification. To me, it's the most magical flower in the world, especially when it transforms and I blow a wish."

Brie picked up the hot cup of tea and took a long sip, closing her eyes as she took in its healing warmth. "Mmm… Thank you, Celestia. For the flower, your wisdom, and this tea. It's exactly what I needed."

"Don't forget the cookies," Faelan added, grabbing two more from the plate.

Celestia bowed and was about to leave the room when Marquis told her in a gentle tone, "Get a cup for yourself. I would like you to join us."

She gave Marquis another quick bow, a lovely smile gracing her face as she looked up at him in adoration. "Thank you, Master."

Taking advantage of her short absence, Marquis addressed Faelan. "There is no reason to worry about Mrs.

Davis."

He turned to Brie and said, "We shall have a long talk, you and I. There is much I do not know, and now that I am becoming personally involved it is imperative I remedy that."

"I will try, Marquis, but it's hard not to get emotional when I talk about everything that's happened. Sometimes it chokes me up so much and nothing comes out."

He raised an eyebrow, pausing for a moment. "To aid you with that, I think you need a session with my flogger."

Faelan could see relief flood through Brie at the suggestion.

"Mr. Wallace, I would like it if you stay to observe. It won't take long."

Faelan was uncertain why Marquis was making such a request, but he respected the Dom far too much not to feel honored.

When Celestia returned with her cup, Marquis took it from her and instructed her to sit beside Brie while he poured her tea.

Faelan appreciated the unique relationship between them. Marquis was a demanding Master, but he always treated Celestia with the utmost respect. Faelan hoped to follow his example one day, but first he needed to find a sub who would appreciate such treatment. Mary would have thought it weak if he had done such a thing.

No, he needed someone with the same strength and emotional grace as Celestia. Finding such a person—*that* was the real challenge.

He glanced at Brie. Even before he began exploring

the lifestyle, his spirit had recognized the submissive in her. Losing Brie to Davis had been a crushing blow, but time had proven the two were a good match. The truth Faelan had to face was that he'd never earned her devotion—her interest, yes, but not her love.

It had taken him a long time to admit it to himself. The moment he realized that, with the help of Marquis Gray's counsel, he'd become free from his obsession with her.

It had allowed him to move forward with Mary. Despite the fact their relationship hadn't ended well, he'd learned through their joint struggles. He was a better man, and Dom, for loving Mary.

Tono Nosaka had helped him see that.

Faelan snorted to himself. Oh, how he'd resented the guy when they were in direct competition for Brie's affection, but now—years later—he held Nosaka in the same high regard as Marquis.

The world was a remarkably complicated place.

He stilled his own musings when he overheard Celestia telling Brie, "If you can find where Rytsar Durov put it, I would deeply appreciate you giving it to Sir Davis yourself."

Faelan noticed Brie flinch at the mention of Durov's name, but she quickly forced a smile and asked, "What should I be looking for?"

"It's a small box with a blue bow."

Brie looked perplexed. "I have no idea where he might have left it, but I will definitely be on the lookout."

"Normally I would just let it go, but this is a very

special gift."

"Do you mind sharing what it is?" Brie asked.

"Not at all," she replied. "I knew it was meant for him the instant I came across it. The tie pin is in the shape of a violin made from vintage watch parts. The woman who created it is a true genius."

"It sounds perfect."

Celestia said excitedly, "You will be as enchanted by it as much as I was."

"I will definitely look for it, Celestia. I promise," Brie said, taking both her hands and squeezing them.

"I'm certain Rytsar Durov knows exactly where it is. He doesn't seem like the kind of man to lose things."

Brie closed her eyes, letting Celestia's hands go as she struggled to keep her emotions in check.

Faelan came to Brie's rescue, asking Marquis, "You mentioned a flogging session, did you not?"

"I did," Marquis replied.

Brie opened her eyes with a hopeful look, but her pleasant expression quickly disappeared when she asked, "Would it be safe for the baby?"

"The impact would only involve your back. It would in no way endanger the child, whereas the emotions you are struggling with may be having a negative impact."

Brie suddenly looked distressed.

"Naturally, I will speak with your husband and seek medical advice before we proceed." Marquis's calm voice seemed to reassure her.

Brie nodded, stating, "I hope we can."

"Celestia, would you mind getting the room ready for us in the event we do?"

"If it pleases you, Master," she answered, but the tentative look Celestia gave to Marquis left Faelan with the impression she was concerned she'd said something wrong.

Marquis put his hand on the top of her head and smiled. "It pleases me greatly, my love." With his reassurance given, Celestia left them to carry out the task he'd given her.

Once she was gone, Marquis turned to them. "I will not be keeping what's happened with Durov from her. While there are some things she must never be told for her own protection, my wife deserves to gather with the community in support of Durov."

Brie nodded, looking like she was about to cry again but trying to put on a brave face.

"No need for tears, Mrs. Davis. Our Russian friend has the strength of an army behind him."

"I agree—an army," Faelan repeated, wanting Brie to know and *believe* they were prepared to rally together to save him.

Flogging Her Pain

Marquis left to make his phone calls, leaving Brie and Faelan alone. He noticed her rubbing her belly and asked, "Has it started moving yet?"

She glanced up at him in surprise, a smile spreading across her lips at the question. "Yes, my baby has." She looked down at her belly. "It feels like a tiny miracle every time that flutter happens."

"My sister said the same thing. She actually enjoyed being pregnant, but near the end she was restricted to bed rest."

"I hope that doesn't happen to me." Brie grasped her stomach with both hands as she spoke to the child, "Hold on, little one. Mommy's doing everything she can to keep you safe." She shook her head, confessing to Faelan, "This poor baby has only known stress from practically the very first moment I found out I was pregnant. The child is doomed…"

Faelan put his arm around her. "No, now that your husband is awake, the tides of your future are changing, and I'm making it my personal mission to help make the rest of your term as stress-free as possible."

"But what about Ry—"

Before she could finish, Celestia walked in to let them know everything was ready. She smiled kindly at Brie and asked, "Go on please. I didn't mean to interrupt. What were you saying?"

Brie glanced at Faelan, somehow able to think quickly on her feet. "I was just about to tell Mr. Wallace I'm worried because I suddenly have a craving for rice and beans. Like I could eat them morning, noon, and night. Is that normal?"

Faelan was impressed, and kept her ruse going, "Well, my sister ate hot dogs nonstop out of the refrigerator. Sometimes she went through an entire package a day."

Celestia shuddered. "Oh, that's awful."

"And the baby turned out all right?" Brie asked, seeming honestly interested.

"Yeah, cutest damn kid. You'd never know Joshua is literally made out of weenies."

Both women laughed, which was what Marquis walked into when he returned.

"What did I miss?" he asked his sub.

"Just the odd cravings of Brie and Mr. Wallace's sister," Celestia answered.

Marquis seemed amused by their conversation. "I have heard women become slaves to certain cravings."

"And Brie's is rice and beans," Celestia told him.

"Rice and beans?" Marquis asked, giving Brie a knowing look.

She shrugged. "I just was wondering if my baby will

be okay despite that."

"If that is your concern, you will be pleased to learn your husband not only encourages the session but your doctor okayed it. Who knows, it may even cure you of your odd craving."

Faelan could see the relief on Brie's face, and was grateful. He knew that this flogging session with Marquis was exactly what Brie and the baby needed if they were to remain unscathed from the tragedy of recent events. Knowing he was being invited to watch the Master at work, Faelan decided to ask the same question he'd been conditioned to ask while attending the Dominant Training course.

"What should I concentrate on as I observe you today, Marquis Gray?"

"A fine question, young Padawan," Marquis answered with a smirk. "I would like you to observe the benefits of pain used for emotional healing."

"I have to admit that is not a direction I've gone before so it should prove quite educational."

Marquis glanced in Brie's direction. "You may have need of it in the future."

Faelan nodded, understanding things were about to get more difficult—for everyone involved.

"Your path is a significant one, Mr. Wallace," Marquis stated. "Not only now, but in the years ahead. I consider it an honor to be a part of it."

Faelan looked at him in humorous disbelief, unsure if the normally subdued Master was having a little fun at his expense—especially after the Star Wars reference.

"That has got to be the biggest compliment ever given," Celestia said in awe, looking at her Master.

"I agree." Faelan chuckled lightly. "Which is why it can't possibly be about me. Nosaka, perhaps…"

Marquis's gaze bore into his soul. "I do not speak idle words."

"Yes, I'm well aware," he replied, flustered by the man's intense scrutiny.

"Rather than deflect my compliment, embrace your God-given talents and commit to using them wisely."

Faelan felt a tremendous responsibility, wanting to live up to Marquis's belief in him, but thought it misplaced. "My talents with particular instruments mean little when I don't possess your wisdom."

Marquis smiled at his answer. "Ah, but you do. You just haven't learned to trust it yet."

Faelan stared at him as a rush of adrenaline coursed through his body.

"You feel it, don't you?" Marquis asked perceptively. "Those things that have held you down will begin to lose their tight grip. Once you are ready to let go, you will be free."

The idea of truly being free of the burdens he carried…it was an intoxicating concept, and Faelan nodded.

Celestia informed Marquis, "The room and your music are ready, Master."

"Excellent."

Marquis put his hand on the small of Brie's back and guided her through the hallways. Faelan followed behind, fascinated by the quiet power of the man. Every interaction was thoughtful and profound. He shook his head, still digesting Marquis's assertion about his future.

They walked to the end of the hall and the Master opened the door, ushering them into a stylish room. Rather than a dark dungeon, the playroom was bright and imaginative, one wall of it covered with a variety of floggers hung in such a way as to make its own artful design. The wall opposite was covered in mirrors that reflected the design.

Every piece of equipment in the room was covered in leather of varying colors, including the St. Andrew's cross.

"I've never been allowed in this room before," Brie said, turning around, awestruck.

"No one has. This is our private playroom," Marquis informed her.

Brie smiled at Celestia and told Marquis, "It's so beautiful."

"Thank you, Mrs. Davis. I believe the environment of a scene is as important as the session itself."

Faelan understood the significance of Marquis allowing them into his private sanctuary and noted every detail. The sheer number and quality of his tools must have cost a small fortune. "I must say, being a man of modest means myself, this is quite impressive."

Marquis walked over to the instrument wall and picked up a black flogger. "This was my first." He handed it to Faelan. "As you can see, even though it has been well used, it remains in fine condition. It's not the number of tools you own, but the quality. Everyone spends their money and time on those things that matter most to them. It has taken me many years to complete this room, but every piece, from the instruments to the furniture, even the décor, reflect my steadfast focus to create this vision."

Faelan studied the room, understanding that what he was seeing was insight into the man's inner soul. "I'm impressed."

Marquis looked at the instrument in his hand. "And it all started with this one flogger. Proof that if you remain true to your vision, nothing is impossible."

Marquis turned his attention to Brie. "Now it is time for you, pearl. Remove your blouse and bra."

Brie quickly took off the two items and bowed at his feet.

"Before we begin, I must ask you to step out for a moment, Celestia."

She bowed to her Master without question and left the room.

"Now tell me, pearl, how were you feeling when you arrived here?"

She looked up at him, her countenance transforming from anticipation to one of pain. "I'm so afraid, Marquis."

"For Durov?"

"Yes."

"And Lilly?"

She bowed her head. "I want to hurt her."

"That is a side of you I have not seen before."

"She wanted to harm my baby. I feel only a red-hot rage toward her."

"This rage has no place to go," Marquis stated. "It is eating you up inside, much like the apprehension you feel for Durov."

Brie nodded, tears spilling from her eyes.

"Negative emotions are only valuable when they can produce change. Otherwise, you must exert your will over them, pearl."

"Yes, Marquis."

Marquis took the flogger from Faelan. "Before you begin a session of healing, it's vital for the submissive to acknowledge her emotions. To overlook this step will render the session meaningless and it will simply become a temporary high with no substance."

"Understood," Faelan said.

Marquis asked Brie, "Do you mind if I instruct him before we start?"

"No, Marquis."

Brie bowed her head, waiting for the two Doms to speak.

It seemed strange to Faelan to find himself in this position—Marquis preparing him to help Brie if things fell apart around her.

Marquis took his responsibility as Brie's former trainer seriously and being a thorough man, he wanted to ensure that, whatever happened with Lilly and Durov, Brie would come through it still whole.

"Normally, I choose music that soothes or excites, but when performing a session of healing, you need a piece that will draw out strong emotions. Your purpose is not to scene, but to minister."

Faelan nodded, appreciating the explanation and clarification.

"Pearl, I want you to absorb the music when it begins."

"Yes, Marquis," she answered, her voice tinged with fear.

Marquis heard that fear and immediately addressed it. "There is no reason to be frightened."

"But it hurts too much already. I don't want to feel any more," she confessed, crossing her hands over her chest as if it were a physical pain.

Marquis's voice was calming as he explained, "I will not take you deeper than you can bear."

She looked up at him, trembling.

"Do not hinder the release."

"Yes, Marquis."

He grazed her cheek with the back of his hand, smiling down at her. "Know that I am here to bring relief."

Her lips trembled, but she managed to say, "Thank you."

Faelan was moved by the trust Marquis had inspired in Brie. He was one of the few Masters who could fulfill that promise.

Marquis called Celestia back in and instructed her to turn on the stereo. Soon an unfamiliar piece of classical music filled the air. Knowing the Dom well, Faelan suspected it must be by Mozart—Marquis's favorite composer.

The music itself was gripping and complex, the dynamic rhythm of it evoking feelings of angst and torment. Faelan looked down at Brie and saw that she was crying, the musical piece pulling at her already raw emotions.

No longer acknowledging Faelan, Marquis concentrated his energies on Brie.

Out of respect, Faelan stepped back to quietly observe the Master at work.

"Let it all out, pearl," Marquis said soothingly.

An anguished sob ravaged Brie's body as a torrent of tears released. Faelan had to look away, feeling her pain as surely as if it were his own.

He glanced at Marquis and saw tears in the man's eyes as well. That's when he realized Marquis was acting as Brie's conduit. Her pain becoming his pain…

The Master hovered over Brie as she became consumed by the excruciating pain of her emotions. In this exchange, he became her guardian, absorbing Brie's release so she would not suffer alone.

Placing one hand on the top of her head and keeping his eyes on her, Marquis reached his hand out. Celestia moved to him, unbuttoning his shirt, and sliding it off his arm. Marquis switched hands so he maintained contact with Brie at all times, while Celestia slipped the sleeve off his other arm. Bare-chested, Marquis turned his palm upward and waited.

Like a practiced surgical nurse, Celestia placed the black flogger on his hand, the same one Marquis had mentioned was his first tool. His fingers grasped it tightly, and with his hand still on Brie, he began flogging himself. Each lash of the flogger leaving red trails on his back.

When he was done, he lifted his hand from Brie and let the falls of the flogger gently graze against the skin on her back.

Suddenly her tears stopped.

"Stand, pearl," Marquis commanded, his voice ragged with pain.

She got on her feet and stretched her arms out in supplication.

Celestia quickly went to her, moving Brie's long hair to the front, baring her back.

Marquis's intense gaze never left Brie as if his connection with her was so strong there was a barrier between them and the rest of the world. He stood back just as the tone of the music began to darken in mood and character.

With a swipe of his arm, he wiped away the tears on his face as he readied himself to deliver the first strike.

Brie stood completely still as if in a trance, waiting for the welcomed stroke of the flogger to release her from the spell.

When Marquis released the first lash, it came hard and fierce.

The skin on Brie's back reverberated in waves from the strength of the impact, but she made no sound. Then came the volley of strokes, each as intense and unforgiving.

Brie bore it in silence—a silence that concerned Faelan.

Instead of release, the pain inside her seemed to build in intensity.

Marquis did not let up, his concentration focused and exacting as he unleashed his healing pain.

Just as Faelan felt the need to intervene, Brie let out a long, agonizing cry to the heavens. "Rytsar!"

Marquis stopped, dropping the flogger to the floor as he encased Brie in his strong arms, squeezing her tight in his steel-like embrace.

The music continued with its dramatic strain, encompassing everyone in the room in the powerful melody.

Faelan glanced at Celestia, who was crying. He was tempted to hold out his hand to her, understanding her need for human contact after the emotional impact of Brie's heart-wrenching cry.

Closing his eyes, Faelan turned all his focus on Brie, wanting to infuse her with positive energy. He felt a stirring in his core, but just as it began to increase the image of Trevor flashed in his mind.

Faelan opened his eyes and was surprised to find Marquis staring directly at him. A gaze so penetrating it almost paralyzed him with its intensity.

Faelan broke eye contact, unnerved by it, and shifted his gaze to Brie. She was facing Marquis, a relaxed expression on her face as she looked up at the Master, oblivious to the world around her.

Faelan suspected she was flying high on endorphins after the intense session, but it was more than that. There seemed a fundamental change in her countenance. What Marquis Gray was able to accomplish with his flogger was unprecedented and breathtakingly powerful so Faelan faced him again, bowing in respect.

Marquis nodded his acknowledgment, then asked, "Mr. Wallace, would you stay with Brie while I speak to my sub?"

Faelan looked in Celestia's direction and saw that she was still crying. "Of course."

Marquis cupped Brie's cheek and leaned down to

kiss her on the forehead before leaving. He then headed to a chest of drawers and pulled out a small vial, handing it to Faelan.

With a gentle touch, Marquis escorted Celestia out, speaking in a soothing tone as they exited the room together.

Faelan guided Brie to a settee in the corner and had her lie down on it with her head resting against his lap. Brie uttered no sound as she complied, then closed her eyes as he began to rub the healing balm on her back, covering the bright red marks with a soothing touch.

As he tended to her aftercare, Faelan was hit by the overpowering responsibility of his vow to her and his duty to Davis.

Certain her Master would want to know when they were finished, Faelan took out his phone and took a quick picture of Brie's back with the text:

Marquis's work.

Within seconds Davis shot back:

Good.

Marquis came back a short time later with Celestia. Faelan was pleased to see her looking like herself again. With gentle care, she helped Brie to her feet so that Marquis could inspect the marks he'd made on her back.

"A fine session," he stated after checking her over.

"Yes, Marquis, thank you," Brie replied breathlessly, still flying on the flood of endorphins.

He looked at Brie with tenderness. "I'm grateful to

see you more at peace."

Marquis then clasped Faelan's shoulder. "Come, join me in the study. I would like to talk about what happened today."

Faelan felt a twinge of unease, wondering if Marquis was going to talk about the meaning behind that look he'd given. As far as Faelan knew, he'd done nothing to disturb the Dom during the observation.

Not wanting to shirk in his duty of aftercare, Faelan asked Brie, "Is there anything you need before I go?"

She looked up at him with those honey-colored eyes and smiled. "No, I am well. I appreciated your care."

He nodded, grateful that the intimate connection of aftercare had not rekindled old feelings within him. He'd finally achieved what Nosaka said was possible—going from passion to friends.

On their way out, Marquis asked Faelan, "Overall, your thoughts of the flogging session?"

"Stunningly powerful."

"As you are probably aware, Mrs. Davis is unusually receptive to such an intense emotional exchange. Not everyone gives in to it as easily."

Faelan nodded, knowing Mary would have fought hard against it. "I will keep that in consideration."

After they were seated in the study, Marquis leaned forward on his desk, his hands laced under his chin as he stared at Faelan with that penetrating gaze from before.

Shifting uncomfortably in his seat, Faelan asked, "Is there something you want from me, Marquis?"

The man's eyes narrowed. "During the most intense part of the scene, I felt a darkness in the room. Do you know what that was from?"

Faelan was honestly perplexed. "I have no idea."

"What were you doing immediately after the flogging ended?"

Faelan had to think back on it. "I recall closing my eyes to concentrate on Brie. I felt the need to share my inner strength with her." He looked at Marquis self-consciously. "Was that foolish?"

"No, it is necessary—essential even—but something happened then, did it not?"

Thinking on it more, Faelan realized he'd forgotten one important detail. Meeting Marquis's gaze, he suddenly felt a rush of fear.

How could the man know my innermost thoughts?

Explaining to Marquis, he divulged, "I had something come to mind, something from my past. It interrupted my focus on Brie."

Marquis pointed his finger at Faelan. "*That* is what holds you back. You will not be good to anyone until you resolve that issue from your past."

His pronouncement hit Faelan hard in the chest. "But I can't undo what happened," he protested. "Are you claiming I have no future as an effective Dominant because of it?"

Marquis sat back in his chair. "You are controlled by that darkness you cradle inside you. Until you come to terms with it, you will never advance. I did not see clearly how bound you truly are until today."

Faelan swallowed down his feelings of defeat. As appointed guardian over Brie, his only focus had to be ensuring her protection. "Thank you for allowing me to observe the session," he stated, abruptly standing up. "I would converse further, but it's important I secure the resources Durov has allotted to me."

Faelan had only one mission—to ensure that Lilly never touched Brie again. It gave him a sense of purpose now that his future as a Dom had been put into question.

"Of course," Marquis agreed, getting up to see him out. "You do what needs to be done, but I caution you not to lose yourself in your execution of it. There is no point in sacrificing your life in an attempt to blot out the past."

It unsettled Faelan how perceptive Marquis was proving to be.

The Plan

"Mr. Wallace, I have it on good authority that Lilly will attempt an escape right after the birth of her child," the man hired to watch over Brie informed him.

"Oh really…" Faelan raised an eyebrow and smiled, pleased that he was being given an opportunity to exact his own brand of revenge on the woman.

"How would you like us to proceed, sir?"

"Let her escape, but we will intercept her. I want that woman to experience a taste of what she had planned for Brie."

"Torture?" His question was asked matter-of-factly.

"Not in the physical sense. You will abduct her after she escapes, but I want her to experience the fear of being hunted down. Drag it out so that she is terrified when you finally capture her."

"When the time comes, it will be my pleasure to do so," he told Faelan, explaining, "Putting brutal people in their place is tremendously satisfying to me."

Faelan nodded, impressed with the men Rytsar had

chosen to serve under him. They seemed to be vigilantes with a strong sense of justice. Men he could relate to.

"Now that I know her plans, I can make arrangements for her next imprisonment." Faelan smiled to himself as he began formulating how he would subdue Brie's greatest threat.

Faelan headed directly to the hospital with the news. He needed to speak to Davis about his ideas. Although what he had in mind was extreme, Faelan was confident he would get Davis's consent once he explained the depth and meaning behind it.

Walking into the hospital room, however, he was confronted with the sight of a camera crew around Davis's bed. He'd unknowingly walked into an interview, given by one of the popular female LA news reporters.

Faelan looked over at Brie, who was in the corner watching. She just shrugged and gestured him to join her where she stood.

"…I know it must have been a terrible shock given what happened yesterday, but let me tell you how happy we are to see you are recovering, Sir Davis. The entire community has been pulling for you ever since the plane crash." The reporter smiled at Thane as she pushed the mic close to his mouth, waiting for a response.

The fierceness in Davis's eyes as he stared into the camera left no doubt of his state of mind, even though his words were only above a whisper. "I demand Rytsar Durov's safe return."

She nodded, her smile disappearing as she agreed. "Hopefully the men who abducted him are watching now. If they are, what would you want to say?"

"No harm or there will be conseque—" He began coughing, so the reporter took the mic back and smiled at the camera.

"In case you didn't get that, you are expected to deliver Rytsar Durov back here unharmed."

Brie started to move toward her husband, obviously concerned for his health, but she stopped when she heard the reporter say, "Sir Davis, you are considered a hero around our news station."

Stepping back beside Faelan, Brie listened with interest.

"After hearing little Lucinda share how you saved her that day, the city was inspired to give you an award for your compassion and bravery."

One of the cameramen handed her a gold plaque, which she promptly displayed in front of the lens before showing it to Davis.

He stared at the reporter with a stunned expression, ignoring the plaque. Tears came to his eyes as he said hoarsely, "She survived?"

The reporter put her hand to her mouth, looking as if she found his reaction adorable. "Oh my, you didn't know? Yes, I'm happy to report that Lucinda is alive and well, Sir Davis."

Davis looked over at Brie for confirmation, as if he didn't believe what he'd heard.

She nodded as she made her way over to him, pushing past the reporter to take hold of his hand. "It's true, Sir. You saved that little girl on the plane. I spoke to Lucinda myself. In fact," Brie said holding his hand tight, "she has been waiting all this time to give you a picture she made."

Davis shook his head slowly, his raw emotion bared for the world to see. "I never imagined she…" He closed his eyes, unable to finish as he swallowed down the lump in his throat.

Naturally, the reporter was thrilled to catch his poignant reaction on film. Her smile was cheesy as she tilted her head and addressed the camera. "Lucinda, honey, if you are watching, you can give that picture to your hero now."

Faelan didn't care for the way the interview was being handled. It lacked respect for Davis and the seriousness of the situation. He grabbed the man holding the camera and pulled him toward the door, saying, "Let's give these two the privacy they need."

Faelan shooed the entire crew out the door and said a curt, "Thank you," as he shut it.

Davis nodded to him in thanks before turning his attention back to Brie. Smiling at her, he said, "She's alive…"

Brie grinned, squeezing his hand. "She only had a broken arm and if you can believe it, Lucinda was able to go home just a few days after the crash."

"That's remarkable."

"It was a miracle, Sir. Her family was so grateful to you…*is* so grateful." She picked up the plaque and looked at it proudly. "You are a true hero."

Davis did not acknowledge the award, reaching to place his hand on Brie's stomach. "My only thought was if that were my daughter, I would want someone to protect her."

Brie clasped her hands over his, her bottom lip trembling.

Faelan felt uncomfortable witnessing their private moment and was about to leave when Mr. and Mrs. Reynolds opened the door and entered the room. Davis's uncle seemed surprised to see Faelan there and instantly stiffened.

Faelan couldn't help wondering if Reynolds thought he held something against the man. Although it *was* Reynolds who'd informed Davis about him breaking protocol when he'd talked to Brie at the tobacco shop after the Collaring Ceremony, that had been years ago—like a lifetime ago.

He never held it against the guy, firmly believing family needed to look out for each other.

To alleviate any lingering misunderstandings Reynolds might still hold, Faelan walked straight up to the man and held out his hand. "It's a pleasure to see you and your wife again."

Reynolds stared at his open palm for a moment before taking it. "I certainly didn't expect to see you here with Thane, Mr. Wallace."

Davis spoke up. "He's been invaluable since Durov's hijacking."

Mrs. Reynolds looked at Faelan with new compassion. "I had no idea you were helping our Thane." She gave Faelan a motherly hug and patted his cheek when she let go, saying, "Such a nice young man."

Brie giggled behind him. Faelan turned, giving her a lopsided grin.

"You two are a welcomed sight," Davis said, looking

at them gratefully.

Faelan appreciated the significance of their visit, but knew the information he needed to share was too sensitive for an audience, even if they were family.

Davis must have noticed Faelan's look of concern. After receiving hugs from both of them, he asked, "Unc, would you mind getting lunch so we can share a meal together? You always stressed the importance of breaking bread and I need that familial connection."

Mr. Reynolds looked from Thane to Faelan. An observant man, he took the hint and replied, "I couldn't agree more. Come, wife, help me create a feast from the offerings at the cafeteria."

Judy's eyes twinkled as she took the arm he held out to her. "Now that's a challenge I gladly accept." As they were walking out, she asked over her shoulder, "Are you coming, dear?"

Brie looked at her husband, who shook his head. "If you don't mind, I'd like to catch up with Faelan a bit more."

"Don't mind at all," Judy replied. "Leave it all to us."

Once they were gone, Faelan pulled up a chair and sat down next to Thane. When he shared Lilly's plans to escape, Davis stated his surprise and concern, "She's leaving the baby in jail?"

"That's what I've been told."

Davis frowned. "Even though I have no ties to the child, I can't help feeling responsible for it."

Brie respectfully disagreed. "The woman is related to you whether we like it or not, which makes this baby part of your bloodline. However…her mistake should not become your responsibility, Sir."

"There is more," Faelan informed them.

Davis shot him a look. "You don't plan to return her to the authorities, do you?"

"No, I'm convinced she would only escape again."

"I one hundred percent agree," Brie stated.

"So tell me your plans then," Davis insisted.

"You may not be aware of this, but Durov set up a recovery clinic for victims of human trafficking."

Davis furrowed his brow, seeming surprised by the revelation. "No, I was not aware."

"I believe he did it for the girl Stephanie, because he put her in charge of the facility."

"The girl he saved in Russia?"

"Correct. She's been in charge of it for over a year and says it has changed her life."

Brie gazed down at the floor, a sad smile on her lips.

"What is it, Brie?" Davis asked.

She looked up at him with tears in her eyes. "I remember when Rytsar read the note Stephanie had written to him. He carries it in his wallet. Back then he wasn't sure how to help her but…I guess he figured out a way."

"My old friend surprises me yet again."

Brie asked Faelan, "Have you spoken to Stephanie yourself? Do you know if she is doing well?"

"I have, actually, and she is doing remarkably well," Faelan told her. "The girl is seriously passionate about what she's doing. If you get the chance to meet her, you'd know what I mean."

Brie smiled to herself. "That makes me very happy."

Davis understood this was a lead-in to Faelan's plan, and asked, "What did you speak to her about concerning Lilly?"

"I want to make sure that woman pays for her deeds in a way that will impact her profoundly. Both Durov and I were agreed on that, although Marquis has been strongly opposed to anything that does not involve the legal system."

"Go on."

"I would like to introduce Lilly to the recovery center in a unique way."

Both Brie and Davis looked concerned, and he could see Brie was about to protest.

"Hear me out before you say anything. I've spoken to Stephanie personally and explained I had a woman whom Durov wanted punished. Without hesitation, she insisted on helping. I did not mention names when I shared with Stephanie some of Lilly's violent history, including what she planned for you," he added, looking at Brie. "While she and I are both agreed that Lilly needs to see firsthand the devastation human trafficking causes the victims and families, we know she cannot be trusted to have any contact with those who are recovering."

"Agreed," Davis growled angrily.

"Therefore, I have assigned guards to watch over her, but I would also like to bring in an 'assistant'. Someone who will act as if she is suffering the same treatment, but who is really there to extract information as Lilly fulfills her role."

"What is her role?" Brie asked.

"She will be in charge of food prep, cleanup, latrine

duty—any menial but necessary job to run the facility. However, she will do it all while isolated from others."

Davis actually smiled but cautioned Faelan, "She is extremely dangerous, not someone to toy with. Who do you plan to 'assist' Lilly?"

"There is someone I have in mind, but I still need to speak with her to see if she's willing. I would share her name but if she agrees, no one can know. It is the only way to protect her identity."

The Reynoldses came bursting into the room with large bags of food.

"What did you do, buy the whole cafeteria out?" Brie laughed.

"Well, we weren't sure what Mr. Wallace likes so we have all the bases covered," Mr. Reynolds explained.

Judy dug into one of the bags and pulled out a large chocolate cake. "The cook there is a complete angel. When I told her what we were doing, she insisted on giving us the whole cake." She walked over to Faelan and handed it to him. "I remembered Brie once said that you like chocolate."

He smirked as he took the massive cake from her. "Thank you, Mrs. Reynolds. I'm not quite sure what to say."

"*I'm going to share* would be nice," Brie suggested.

Mrs. Reynolds whispered to Faelan, "You aren't required to share."

"Good to know," he joked. Setting the cake on a counter, he helped Mrs. Reynolds unpack the rest of the food containers. While they were busy unpacking, Davis addressed his uncle.

"Unc, Mr. Wallace just shared something that has me deeply concerned."

"What's that, Thane?" he asked, walking over to him.

"Lilly plans to abandon her child."

"What?!" Judy cried, turning around, a horrified look on her face. "How can a mother do that?"

"What will happen to the child if she does such a thing?" Reynolds demanded, clearly upset.

"I assume the child becomes a ward of the state until a suitable foster home is found."

The Reynoldses stared at each other, communicating between themselves.

Thane continued, "I do not think the child's fate should be left to the state."

"Absolutely not," Mr. Reynolds agreed.

"However, raising the child guarantees involvement with the mother at some point. It would be inevitable."

Faelan noticed the terrified look in Brie's eyes. He sincerely hoped Davis wasn't going to suggest Brie raise Lilly's child.

Mr. Reynolds glanced at Judy again, who responded by nodding. "I think we may have a solution, Thane."

Judy walked over to her husband and held his hand, announcing, "We would love to adopt Lilly's baby."

Davis cautioned, "You must understand the risk. This isn't something that should be decided lightly."

Mr. Reynolds put his hand on his nephew's shoulder. "Lilly is my niece by blood and the grandchild of my sister. I feel it is my duty to bring love into this innocent's life."

"Lilly could ruin you, Unc."

Mr. Reynolds stepped back, putting his arm around his wife. "Judy and I are tough old birds. I think we can handle it."

Judy was actually beaming. "Thane, you know how much I've always wanted to be a mother. Now I will get that chance! And for a child who desperately needs us."

Brie was staring at the two of them with a mixture of joy and misgiving as she unconsciously rubbed her own belly.

Faelan understood Brie's mixed emotions. As long as Lilly lived, no matter how happy the Reynoldses were as a family, they would have a dark cloud hovering over their future. But it relieved Faelan to know that Brie was not the one being asked to take on that responsibility.

Faelan was certain that Davis also shared Brie's misgivings. As innocent as Lilly's child was, it carried with it a terrible curse.

"So that's settled," Mr. Reynolds announced proudly. "The baby will remain with family."

"If you are decided, I can have Thompson contact you. You'll need to have all the paperwork ready in preparation of the baby's arrival."

"Won't they get suspicious if we jump in to claim the child before she actually gives it up?" Judy asked, sounding worried.

"Of course not," Mr. Reynolds explained to her. "It's only natural for family members to seek custody of a child when the mother is in custody."

"Just as long as we don't hurt our chances of adopting the baby," she stated, smiling at Thane.

"I would never jeopardize the adoption," Davis assured her. "Thompson is one of the best in the legal arena. He'll advise you on exactly what you need to do."

Judy looked down at her arms dreamily, pretending to cradle the infant. "I feel a connection now that I know the baby needs us." She let out a happy sigh and went back to piling up food on plastic plates. "And now we are going to feast in celebration of Thane's recovery!"

Faelan still needed confirmation that his plans were acceptable to Davis and asked, "So are we in agreement about the rest?"

Davis motioned him closer and said, "I'm confident you will do what's best."

Taking Brie's hand, he looked at his wife. "But I want to know what you think, babygirl?"

She glanced at Faelan and smiled. "I have confidence in you as well."

Faelan took the overstuffed plate of food Judy offered him. The damn thing was weighed down with all manner of food, but he ate with gusto. Now that permission had been given…

Lilly wouldn't know what hit her.

Best Woman for the Job

Faelan rang the doorbell and waited. He wished it hadn't come to this, but he felt without a doubt she was the best person for the job.

It was worth the indignity he was about to endure.

Mary, being Mary, naturally took her time to answer the door. When it finally opened, Faelan saw the irritation on her face quickly turn to shock as she recognized who was standing in front of her. She tried to slam the door, but he had anticipated her reaction and deftly stuck his foot out to block it.

"Get the fuck out of here, Faelan!" she screamed.

"Just hear me out."

"And why the hell would I do that?"

"Because I'm not here for me."

Those sensual lips of hers turned downward into an ugly frown. "What the fuck does that mean?"

"Brie needs help."

Rather than inspiring her sympathy, Mary's face contorted in anger. "Don't you dare give me a guilt trip about not going to visit her. You have no right. No right at all!"

"Guilting you is not my aim, Mary."

Her frown grew more severe. "You know as well as I do that the last thing Brie needs is a fuck-up like me in her life."

"I'm not asking you to be a part of it."

"What then?" she demanded, her voice rising in pitch along with her fury.

"I need your help in handling a dangerous situation that involves Brie. You happen to have the skills required for the task."

Mary's tone became condescending. "Oh, I see. This is your pathetic way of trying to win me back or something."

His amiable smile did not falter when he told her, "I would never take you back."

"Hah! You're still in love with me and you know it."

"I was—once. But you were very effective in your exit. I hold no romantic feelings toward you now."

Her sarcastic laughter filled the air. "I don't believe it."

"Look in my eyes and know the truth," he insisted.

Mary couldn't hide her arrogant smile as she gazed deep into his blue eyes. Her haughtiness slowly faded as she studied him longer. Eventually a look of concern flashed across her face but she quickly masked it with a smirk, stating, "You're like a dog—loyal and begging for its master, no matter how it's treated."

Faelan held back a surge of resentment, knowing that what he was about to share would rock that fragile confidence of hers.

"I'm loyal, yes. I am also a Dominant. I know my limit and you crossed it. I told Brie once that I am a man of extremes. I'm either hot or cold toward a person. While I've matured since then, the essence of that statement still holds true. When I was in love with you, I would have done anything for you. Now that you've destroyed those feelings, there's no bringing them back. We will always be connected because of the history we share, but I can guarantee you one thing, Mary. I will never love you again."

Those last words hung in the air between them.

She said nothing, but her gaze returned to his for several moments. Mary eventually leaned back against the doorframe and began clapping her hands together slowly. "Nice speech. I'll give you an eight out of ten for that one."

Having no interest in playing games, Faelan directed the conversation back to the reason he'd come. "Let me enter and I will tell you the details. As I said before, there is a high level of risk involved should you choose to help."

Although he knew that fact actually intrigued her, she asked in a dismissive tone, "Why the hell would I put myself at risk for you?"

"Not me—Brie."

Mary pursed her lips. She considered Brie family, and Faelan suspected those fighter instincts were already rising up inside her even as they spoke.

His suspicions were confirmed when she opened the door farther, turning away from him as she started down the hall. "Don't get your hopes up. I haven't agreed to anything."

"Of course not," he replied, entering her apartment and shutting the door behind him.

"In fact, I'm not doing a damn thing for you," she added as an extra jab.

Faelan chuckled to himself. Her brittle responses were in high form, but they'd lost the power to provoke him.

Looking around her apartment, he noted all the carefully placed Disney memorabilia. Faelan understood the importance of each item's placement. Mary had painstakingly set them in the perfect spots to complement the room. It was serious business to her.

When he spotted the jeweled necklace he'd given her, displayed in a prime location, he was left to ponder. Did the placement signify the uniqueness and worth of the item or did it hint to her lingering feelings for him?

The possibility that she regretted her actions disturbed Faelan. It would be sadly ironic if she spent the rest of her life secretly pining for him after being so brutal in her breakup.

Mary noticed him staring at the necklace and quickly pushed him toward the small kitchen. "You want something to drink?"

"Water would be fine."

"Whatever…" She got a glass out of the cupboard and poured a generous amount of rum into it, before topping it off with a splash of Coke. She then grabbed another glass and filled it with tap water. Sliding the glass across the kitchen table to him, she picked up her own glass and sat down.

Faelan stared at her as he slowly took a drink, trying to decide where to begin. "So, did you hear about the Russian?"

She snorted. "Of course, it was all over the news. Must have flipped Brie out to be right there when it happened. I hope he was granted a quick death, poor bastard."

Mary took a long draught from her glass.

"I am choosing to believe he's alive until I hear otherwise," Faelan replied, finding her pessimistic attitude offensive. "Durov was here in LA to protect Brie. The moment he was taken, it put her back in danger."

He suddenly had Mary's attention. "Protect her from what?"

"Whom," he replied.

"It's that bitch, isn't it? Like mother like daughter…"

Faelan nodded, impressed Mary had been so quick to figure it out.

"So where is she now?"

"Lilly is planning to escape from jail."

Mary sat back in her chair, huffing angrily. "I call bullshit. How could you possibly know that?"

"Durov set me up with the manpower to keep accurate tabs on Lilly. It's essential for Brie's protection. I know for a fact that she's planning to break out after the baby is born."

"And what does any of this have to do with me?"

"I'm taking her to a secret location, but I need someone beside her at night who won't raise suspicion."

"What? Are you seriously are asking me to play nanny to the cunt?"

"You would be acting as my informant, as well as ensuring Brie is kept safe from her wrath."

"Hey, here's an idea…why not off the bitch and be done with it?"

"Brie refuses to consider it."

Mary leaned toward him, stating in a sarcastic voice, "Then you simply don't tell her."

"I agreed to play by her rules, just as Durov was forced to."

Mary rolled her eyes. "But killing the bitch is much less complicated."

Faelan smirked.

"So what exactly are you expecting me to do with the cunt?"

"It's a lengthy commitment, I won't lie."

"What kind of commitment?"

"She'll be kept busy during the day. However, at night I want her to feel utterly alone—except for the one girl on the other side of the wall. Your job will be to commiserate with her, become Lilly's sounding board and give her validation. Your primary goal will be to get her to open up about what happened with Brie without raising suspicion. I need to know if what she tells you lines up with what she confessed to Durov."

"What exactly did she do to Brie? Last I heard they had a falling-out in China and all ties were cut between them." Her eyes narrowed. "Don't tell me she came knocking when she thought Sir Davis was on the verge of dying."

"It goes far deeper than that…but no matter what she confesses, don't lose your cool and keep her talking.

It's imperative we find out Lilly's future plans for Brie and her child. You won't be able to do that unless she's convinced you're on her side."

Mary frowned. "Okay, tell me what the hell she wants with Brie's baby."

Faelan felt a low-boiling rage in the pit of his stomach when he told her. "Lilly wanted to abort Brie's baby, and I'm convinced she still plans harm to the child."

"I'll fucking cut the bitch right now," Mary growled, her nostrils flaring. "*No one* hurts the innocent!"

"Our only job is to exact justice."

Mary smashed her fist into her palm. "Oh, I'll show her justice."

Faelan placed his hand on Mary's shoulder to calm her and subconsciously noted as a Dom that she did not pull away from the contact. It was telling.

"Mary, it's important that you understand that Marquis is involved as well. We must measure every action."

"Why is he involved?"

"Durov came to Marquis first seeking assistance with Lilly, but I happened to be there."

"Rytsar never did like you," she needlessly reminded him.

"That's irrelevant at this point. Marquis is convinced Lilly is mentally ill and deserves mercy despite Durov's belief that she is sane and knows exactly what she is doing."

"Whether she is or isn't doesn't matter in my opinion. When a dog is mad you have to put it down."

"Our primary focus is to ensure she doesn't hurt anyone, but Marquis still insists she be treated with care."

"He is mistaken, Faelan. Bitches like that only understand one thing—eat or be eaten."

"But having Marquis involved means our hands are tied."

"Let's back up a moment. You mentioned I would be needed at night. You *do* realize I have a life. What kind of time commitment are we talking here?"

"It will only require a few hours each night but for how long I can't say. I envisioned you coming in, talking to her between the wall each night before heading home to your own bed. When you leave, she'll just assume you've fallen asleep."

"Doesn't sound difficult or risky. Why did you insinuate it's dangerous?"

"Because Lilly is dangerous. If she comes to distrust you, Mary, you *will* become her next target."

"This isn't my first rodeo, you know. I think I can handle the cunt."

"It's the reason I came to you."

"I still haven't agreed to anything yet," she insisted. Mary got up to pour herself another drink. "But the timing couldn't be better really," she told him. "Greg has an upcoming role he's planning to cast me in. This could prove the perfect case study for the psycho bitch I'll be playing."

Faelan couldn't miss the intimate tone in which she'd said the producer's name, letting him know the true nature of their relationship. There was no doubt the man was enjoying Mary's many talents, but it remained to be seen who was using whom.

"If the experience can be used to your advantage,

that's certainly a bonus. However, I'm warning you, Lilly is not to be underestimated—ever."

Mary turned around holding her drink up, a sly grin on her lips. "She ain't met me yet."

Faelan could tell she was already contemplating the things she wanted do, so he warned her again. "Mary, if things get ugly with her, I'm the *only* one allowed to get my hands dirty."

She shrugged.

"I'm serious. It ends here if you don't agree."

"What does it matter to you if I muck my hands a little?"

"Promise me, Mary."

"Fuck you. She went after the only friend I have. Surely I'm owed a swing or two."

He glared at her, unwilling to let it pass until he had her verbal agreement.

"Fine," she spat.

"Fine, as in you won't touch her?"

"Yes, Faelan. You can strangle the bitch with your own hands, but I'll be on the sidelines telling you how to do it."

"Of course, you will," he replied with a smirk, remembering how much he enjoyed her feisty spirit.

"So, I guess I'm in then. I'll let Greg know I'm studying for the part."

"No one can know," Faelan stated emphatically.

"How the hell am I supposed to explain to Greg why I can't see him at night?"

"You're a resourceful girl. I'm sure you'll figure something out."

She played with the glass, running her fingertip over the rim in a sensual motion. "Last thing I want is for him to think I'm sneaking behind his back to be with my ex-Master."

Was she trying to flirt with him? The balls of that woman…

"You won't have to worry about that," Faelan said, standing up to end their conversation. Holding out his hand to her, he said curtly, "I'll call once Lilly is in my custody and is settled in."

"Where are you taking her?"

"Someplace she can learn compassion."

"Good luck with that," she answered sarcastically.

When Faelan started toward the door, Mary reached out to stop him. "Look, even though it ended badly between us, I have to admit it's good seeing you again."

The vision of her collar in the trash came to mind, and he pushed past her.

No matter what Mary thought this would involve, Faelan had made certain the two of them would have as little contact as possible. He doubted she understood the damage she'd done—but her ruthlessness was something he would never forget.

Dangerous Lover

Faelan had become a bit obsessed with the elusive woman at the Haven who watched him in the shadows but never made a move to connect. She'd been watching him from afar for weeks now.

His mysterious admirer looked to be a few years older than he was, and deliciously curvy—the kind of curves that called to the animal in him. It was surprising too, because she wasn't his normal fare, but there was something about this woman that beckoned to his primal instincts.

To satisfy his growing desire, he asked one of the subs, raven, to seek her out, instructing her to, "Start a conversation describing a scenario you've written for the box that we've played out together. Ask her what fantasy she would want to put in there. Write down whatever she says afterward, and hand it to me. I'm interested to see where her fantasies lie."

"It would be my pleasure, Faelan," raven replied, giving him a winsome smile and quick bow before running off to do his task.

Faelan watched covertly as the two women talked. They had a long conversation that involved an abundance of laughter. He was unsure how to interpret that, but seeing her smile stirred something inside him.

He knew the woman, but he couldn't place how.

Raven came sauntering back to him with a pleased grin, placing the folded paper in his hand as she continued past, stating in a seductive voice, "Have fun with this one, Faelan."

He opened the note and read:

Her name is Kylie.

Fantasy:
I would like to be tied up so that I am wide open and completely vulnerable to Todd. I want him to tease me with his favorite instruments. It's simple really, I want to know his Dominant touch and not be able to do anything about it.

Faelan looked in Kylie's direction. The name didn't ring a bell, but she'd addressed him by his given name. Did that mean she'd met him before he became a Dominant, or was she one of the groupies who followed him after the documentary released?

He wasn't sure, but he was about to find out.

Faelan watched her as she became engaged in a discussion with a small group of submissives. He enjoyed the fact she was unaware he was staring at her, figuring turnabout was fair play.

Her fantasy would be easy enough to plan out since

she had requested his favorite tools and hadn't mentioned any role play elements.

Folding her request and putting it in his pocket, he strolled off to the alcove he had reserved for the night, smiling to himself as he passed by Kylie's little group who were chattering away.

Little did she know what she was in for…

As was his ritual, Faelan rapped on the metal pole twice with the cane and waited for the gathering.

It was with added enjoyment that he shared the fantasy he had chosen that night. Since Kylie preferred to stay in the back, he spoke a little louder than usual.

"I have selected a rather self-indulgent request tonight. You see, there is a sub in the audience I've had my eye on for a while. Tonight, I will be playing out her fantasy…"

He pulled out the note and read it, making a few changes in the wording. "This sub would like to be tied up so she is completely vulnerable to my favorite instruments." He saw Kylie perk up. Staring directly at her, he continued, "She also stated 'I want to know his Dominant touch and not be able to do anything about it.'"

Kylie stared at him with a stunned expression as the other subs in the crowd looked at her with envy.

"Would you step forward and join me?" Faelan asked, holding out his hand to her.

Kylie's eyes widened, but she didn't make a move.

Faelan cocked his head and smiled, waiting patiently.

Kylie approached him slowly, looking like a deer caught in the headlights. He kept his gaze on her, making sure they didn't lose eye contact. When she was close enough, he took her hand to pull her to him.

The moment their skin touched she audibly gasped.

Leaning in, he asked in a low whisper, "Do you really want to scene with me tonight or should I let you go?" Faelan watched her intently, wanting to see her unspoken reaction.

A rosy blush colored Kylie's cheeks as she met his direct gaze. "I…I…" she stammered as she nervously played with a lock of her brown hair.

"It's okay to say no. I did just hijack your fantasy."

Laughing, she replied, "I wondered why raven suddenly had an interest in my fantasies."

Faelan winked at her. "I decided you've been avoiding me for long enough."

Kylie let out a nervous peal of laughter, but he noticed that her gaze kept drifting back to his lips.

"So, is that a yes?"

Kylie looked into his eyes and asked in disbelief, "Is this really happening?"

Faelan nodded.

"Then yes…Faelan." She said the name as if it were a forbidden word she was terrified to speak aloud.

"I'm not going to bite—too hard," he growled lustfully. Putting his finger under her chin, he lifted her head. "There is no reason to be shy around me."

"Except that you're Faelan."

"Just another Dom," he countered.

She shook her head. "No, I've been watching you."

"I know you have."

Kylie blushed a deeper shade of red.

"I'm curious why you never came up to introduce yourself."

She glanced away, suddenly looking embarrassed. "I'm older than you and never was your type."

"Never? Am I correct to assume we've met before, because I thought you seemed familiar."

Her eyes grew wide, but she did not answer his question.

Faelan looked at the waiting crowd, knowing they were anxious for him to begin.

He put his arm on the small of her back and turned her away from the group, asking quietly, "Would you prefer to discuss this after the scene?"

"Yes. Yes, I would," she answered, seeming exceedingly pleased by the suggestion.

Faelan found that curious and was prompted to ask, "Is there a reason you don't want me to know?"

Kylie shook her head, laughing. "No, but I will say that you're not at all what I was expecting."

Faelan smirked. "Why? What were you expecting?"

"I'd rather not jinx this, but I promise to tell you later."

He couldn't get over the fact she obviously knew him but he could not, for the life of him, remember who she was.

Faelan guided her into the alcove, saying, "Naturally, you have your safewords you can call should you want me to stop."

"Yes, Faelan." She looked up at him and giggled. "I can't believe we're doing this."

He raised an eyebrow. "You've got my curiosity piqued, but now it's time for you to strip."

Her smile faltered. "Strip? Like you're talking *all* my clothes?"

"Is that a hard limit for you?"

"No," she said with a smile, "but I've never been asked to do that before."

"Then this will be a first of many firsts I suspect," he growled seductively.

Kylie suddenly stiffened and whispered in his ear, "I do have a hard limit though."

He smiled. "Of course, lay it on me."

"I don't want to…you know."

Faelan looked at her questioningly. "I'm not a mind reader," he chided with a grin.

"Do *it*."

Faelan had to stop himself from laughing. "You mean *it* as in intercourse?"

Her blush intensified as she nodded.

"I wasn't going to assume that level of intimacy since you didn't state it in your fantasy, but thank you for the clarification."

Kylie let out a sigh of relief. "Okay, now that that's out of the way, give me a minute to get back in my headspace before I fulfill the first task."

"By all means," Faelan replied, standing back to watch.

When Kylie closed her eyes, he noticed after several seconds there was a change in her posture and the expression on her face. When she opened her eyes again, she exuded calmness and poise—no longer the nervous, blushing girl she'd been just moments before.

Her eyes now shone with inner excitement as she began to slowly undress for him.

The woman embraced her submission and was inviting his masculine desire. It was a heady power—receiving such a gift.

Faelan watched as each piece of clothing was taken off, exposing her body to him in parts. First that fleshy ass he'd wanted to spank for quite some time, then those shapely calves that tapered down to her delicate feet with toenails painted an alluring midnight blue. Then she removed her shirt, exposing her feminine stomach. He waited with anticipation as she reached back and undid her bra, letting it fall slowly from her incredibly large and supple breasts—all natural with no need of enhancement.

Kylie folded her clothes and put them in a neat pile before standing before him, her chin held at a confident but respectful angle. The pride she took in exposing her body honored him as a Dom. He wasn't interested in a wallflower; he needed a partner who understood her own beauty and proudly shared it with him and anyone else who might watch.

Faelan wanted everyone here tonight to crave her the way he craved her.

Being able to move an audience emotionally during play turned out to be a special talent of his that he had honed over the years. He could involve them in his scene with a glancing look, a few carefully chosen words, or a lingering caress that caused goosebumps on not only his submissive but those who were watching.

Whether his audience was composed of Dominants or subs, he was able to draw them in naturally while remaining focused on his partner.

"I love the lines of your body. They beg for my lusty attention."

Kylie looked down, a faint smile on her lips indicating her pleasure at his praise.

Faelan remained where he was and commanded, "Sit on the wooden chair I've so thoughtfully placed out for you."

She immediately turned and walked over to the chair, her fine ass swaying back and forth. He let out a low growl so everyone would know what he thought of her magnificent backside.

After she sat down, Faelan picked up some rope and smiled at her hungrily as he approached, speaking loud enough for everyone observing to hear, "Since we have never scened together, you may find I am a little more dangerous than you were expecting."

Now the other Dominants were anticipating the power play between two strangers, while the submissives were imagining the thrill of first encounters.

So easy to draw them in…

Faelan knelt on one knee beside the chair and instructed her, "You will keep your eyes on me at all times. I want you to see what I am doing to this wicked body of yours."

Kylie met his gaze, her breath increasing as she answered, "Yes, Faelan."

He smiled, liking the sound of his name on her lips.

Grasping her ankle tightly, Faelan held it against the leg of the chair. Reaching around, he looped the rope and pulled it through itself, securing her to the wood. Moving up to her calf, he repeated the process, then above her knee, and finally the flesh of her thigh.

"Color?" he asked.

Kylie glanced down at her left leg, bound tightly enough that the rope would leave marks. "Green."

"Not too tight?" he confirmed.

She smiled and shook her head.

He gently caressed her right knee, giving her a lustful look just before he forced her legs wide. The abruptness of the movement caused her to gasp as he spread her wide open for the audience. Holding her other ankle against the wood, he began the same process, tying it just as tight.

When he was done he informed Kylie, "There is nothing you can do now if I want to touch you…" he placed his hand hovering over her bare mound, "here."

Kylie instinctively closed her eyes, waiting for his touch, but he remained still until her eyes opened and her gaze returned to him.

"I'm sorry," she whispered.

Faelan said nothing as he lightly grazed the skin covering her clit. Kylie let out a soft moan, her whole body trembling as she accepted the intimate touch.

He followed up the touch by leaning down and showering her clit with a warm breath of air.

Kylie whimpered in response.

His teasing was just getting started. Getting back to

his feet, he pulled out another length of rope from his bag. Moving behind her, he ordered her to clasp her hands behind her back.

When she did, her breasts naturally lifted, showing them off nicely to the crowd. Faelan tied her wrists together. He bound them to the back spindle of the chair and pulled tightly.

"Color?"

"Yellow," she answered, her voice sounding strained.

He loosened the rope and asked again, "Color?"

"Green. Much better."

Finishing the tie, he reached around her front and began playing with her erect nipples, pinching them lightly before giving them each a playful tug.

"Look at my hands as I play with you," he commanded, this time grabbing each of her massive breasts in his palms and marveling at how amazing they felt in his hands. "I like that you are more than a handful, an abundance of succulent flesh for me to enjoy."

Wrapping his hand around one, he squeezed and forced the nipple to protrude. He then lightly flicked and rubbed the erect nub, knowing that he was sending currents of sexual electricity to her pussy.

Kylie squirmed in her bonds but could not move as he relentlessly caressed and teased her breasts.

"How wet can I make you?" he asked, his voice gruff with unsated desire.

She moaned, watching helplessly as he played with her.

But he wanted more.

Leaning over the chair, he lifted her ample breast to

his mouth and began suckling her nipple. His cock ached with need as he began sucking harder, rolling the other nipple in between his fingers.

Fuck…he wanted her.

Taking a needed break, he stood up and walked back over to his bag, relishing the fact that everyone could see the hard-on he had for her.

Faelan pulled his knife from the bag and held it up for the crowd to see. He smiled evilly as he turned around and approached Kylie with it in his hand.

Her eyes darted to the weapon and she let out what seemed like a frightened whimper. Not knowing her sounds yet, he asked her color.

Her eyes met his for a moment and she said, "Green," but her gaze went right back to the blade.

He definitely had her attention now.

"Have you ever experienced knife play?"

She shook her head.

"Another first," he growled.

Circling around her slowly, Faelan told her, "I enjoy the thrill of edge play. The element of danger is an aphrodisiac for me." He leaned down and touched the tip of the blade against her throat. "Shall we find out if it is for you as well?"

"Yes…" she breathed out.

He pulled her head back to expose her throat and growled huskily. Slowly dragging the dull side of the blade against her skin, he left a trail of white, marking its travel.

Kylie held her breath, her eyes riveted on him.

Faelan lifted the blade and watched as she took in a

deep breath, her gaze now fixed on the instrument he held in his hand.

"I wonder how your pussy will handle it."

"Oh my God."

Faelan grabbed the chair forcibly and slid it into a new position, causing her to cry out in surprise. Now she faced sideways, giving those watching a new angle to enjoy. It also emphasized her helplessness, reminding her that she was completely at his mercy.

Kneeling in front of the chair, Faelan said nothing as he laid the blade flat on her thigh and began to tease her glistening pussy, already wet with need. "I see how my attention excites you." He looked up from between her legs. "I think we may be a good match."

Kylie only nodded.

He knew she was concentrating on the weight of the knife lying on her thigh, wondering how he would use it on her.

To prolong the expectancy of his sub and the audience, he spent his time teasing her clit with the tip of his tongue. Everything he did was meant only to excite, to build her desire as well as that of those who were observing. Satisfaction would only come when *he* was ready.

Faelan leaned back from her to study her bare pussy again, now more red and swollen as it reacted to his intimate kisses.

Spreading her outer lips, he exposed her sensitive clit. "Has anyone ever opened you this way?"

"No," she said with bated breath.

"How does it make you feel?"

"Vulnerable."

"Good."

He felt her tense as he picked up his blade and held it near her clit.

"Have you ever wanted to feel a sharp blade against it?"

She took her eyes off the knife and hesitated for a moment before nodding.

"Then this will be another first for you."

Kylie watched, her whole body now trembling as he lowered the blade tip and pressed it against the protective hood.

She gasped in fear, so he asked, "Would you like me to press harder?"

Her gaze transfixed, she whispered, "Yes."

Faelan watched the muscles of her opening clench as he used a delicate hand, pressing a little harder—enough to provide pressure but not enough to cut. Blood play was not allowed at the Haven, and being her first time, it would not have been wise.

She swallowed hard when he released the pressure, but her eyes shone with lustful excitement.

"I wish to mark you."

"Where?"

"My choice."

Her whole body shuddered and her breathing increased, her fear almost palpable as she watched his dangerous blade.

"Your body…is mine," he informed her as he dragged the sharp end of the blade against her thigh with enough pressure to cut the first few layers without breaking the skin.

She cried out as he made three distinct lines on her pristine skin.

Kylie threw her head back as the euphoria of the edge play took over. That's when he struck—laying down the knife, he encased her clit with his mouth and started sucking as he eased his middle finger into her hot pussy and played with her G-spot.

Kylie hadn't expected the double onslaught as she was still riding the rush of the knife play and couldn't stop the orgasm that overtook her.

He heard the shuffling of feet as the others observing responded to her cries of animalistic passion. Music to his ears…

After he coaxed a second orgasm from her, he pulled away to stare down at his handiwork. The raised skin on her thigh was in the shape of a white F that would later turn a lovely shade of pink.

Untying her slowly, he let Kylie revel in the calmness that comes after intense fear mixed with pleasure, all the while complimenting her on the beauty of each body part as he released her from the rope.

She was like a rag doll when he picked her up to the applause of those attending.

He did not acknowledge it, concentrating instead on the submissive in his arms. A mysterious woman whose identity he was about to discover.

His Commitment

Faelan carried her through the moving crowds to the back rooms of the Haven reserved for private sessions. He took Kylie to the first open room and laid her on the bed, lighting candles and turning on low music to help ease her back down.

Joining Kylie on the bed, he lay facing her so he could run his fingers over her skin as he looked at her face.

She opened her eyes and smiled back at him in pure sub-high contentment.

"You liked it," he stated with a grin as he drew concentric circles on her stomach.

"You're dreamy…" she replied, then her face screwed up in a look of confusion, and she asked, "Am I dreaming?"

"No." He chuckled. "And you have my mark to prove it."

Kylie looked down at her thigh and smiled. "Oh, I'm yours."

"Temporarily," he stated.

"I can't believe I scened in public naked."

"And you liked it."

She blushed and crinkled her nose, confessing, "I did, didn't I?"

He remembered being surprised the first time he had admitted to himself that he was an exhibitionist—after a lifetime of actively avoiding the world at all costs.

It had been incredibly empowering when he'd met Brie and saw the joy in her eyes as she played in front of others. Her total lack of shame inspired him in those early sessions of Dominant Training.

Heck, the two of them had been extremely compatible sexually as Dom/sub; he just hadn't realized it took more than that to keep her as a sub. It had been a hard, but valuable lesson.

It turned out that Mary, however, did not need love in the mix. In fact, she violently opposed it. He'd learned a hard lesson there as well.

His plan had been to keep all interactions void of emotion now that he was back in LA, and yet…he could already tell Kylie was going to be a problem.

She took in a deep breath and sighed in bliss. "Todd Wallace really is the whole package. Football star, movie star, and Dominant extraordinaire."

He looked at her suspiciously. "Why mention football? I haven't played that since I was a kid."

Kylie reached out, wanting to caress his cheek, but stopped and let her hand fall. "You were the best, Todd."

Faelan suddenly felt a cold chill and pulled away from her. "Who are you?"

She lifted her head, resting it on her hand so she could look at him, still flying on endorphins. "It's just me, Kylie. That girl in your geography class at Wiley High that you never paid attention to."

He frowned, still having no recollection of who she was, but not wanting to confront a person who actually might know him from back then. It was unwanted so he denied his past. "I have no idea what you are talking about."

"Sure you do. I saw you every day for a whole year from the back of the class. I was a senior stuck taking a sophomore class because of a few missing credits. Totally humiliating."

"I don't remember you," he insisted. "And I'm certain I would have, considering my attraction to you now."

She blushed. "Well, I'm flattered. I may have been shyer back then, but I was pretty much the same. I'm not surprised you can't remember though. You were the quarterback of the winning football team. I don't think you noticed anyone outside your social circle. Not that I held it against you. I mean, you were a popular guy and I was a second chair flutist. Not exactly the same social status," she said with a laugh.

The cold realization that she knew who he was meant she also knew what he had done. After all these years, did she want to make him pay as well? Would it ever end?

"Don't tell me you were Trevor's girlfriend and have come to exact your revenge on me."

"Are you kidding? That guy was a total dick."

"What are you talking about? He was head of the class and on his way to being valedictorian. The kid was a genius."

Kylie shrugged. "I don't care how smart Trevor was, he was a real asshole to me."

"Well, I don't remember him that way and I think it's disrespectful to speak of the dead when they can't defend themselves."

"His parents certainly did," she huffed. "I couldn't believe what they put you, and your family, through after the accident."

Just the mere mention of Trevor's name had those last moments flashing though his mind.

"I made a mistake and he paid for it. There's really nothing more to be said," Faelan snarled.

"Look, I'm not trying to dredge up the past. It's just that…" She gazed at him with those soft brown eyes, and for a moment he felt lost in them. "The Fishers were brutal to you after their son's death."

"They were reacting to the untimely loss of their son."

"What they did was punish you for an accident. It was wrong and I found it disgusting."

"Nobody felt that way but you, the entire town made that very clear. Maybe you were just blind to the truth."

"Nobody wanted to suffer the wrath of the Fishers after what they did to your family."

"Not true. All those hateful words and actions came from people my family thought of as friends—because of me. You didn't hear the things that were said, but I remember every word. They are all burned into my brain.

The Fishers were only a conduit for it. I was the catalyst. Me."

Kylie shook her head. "I don't think you know what really happened, Todd. I guarantee that your friends felt threatened and were not allowed to show you any sympathy."

Faelan snarled in disgust. "I don't understand the point of bringing *any* of this crap up."

She groaned. "I knew this would make you uncomfortable, and I hated to say anything, but I couldn't just let this go. You need to know you weren't hated. People understood it was an accident. I promise, if you came back you would know I'm telling the truth."

"I'm never going back there," he growled angrily. "It's taken me this long just to get past it."

Kylie smiled at him sadly. "But I don't think you *are* past it."

Faelan was thrown off by the fact Kylie was a part of everything he hated in his past. Yet, despite that, he was still attracted to her. Was he a glutton for punishment or a masochist when it came to love?

Rather than dwell on feelings he couldn't afford, Faelan poured his energy into helping Thane and Brie.

"I'm glad you're here," Davis said as soon as he entered the room. "Things have just become much more complicated. Durov's brothers have decided not to get involved. After everything he's done for them… Those men owe him their very lives!" His anger only resulted in a flurry of coughs that left him breathless and weak.

Brie hovered over him, trying to get him to drink some water, but it only infuriated the man and he yelled at her in frustration. She threw the cup against the wall and stormed out of the room.

Silence followed her exit.

"I can't help him. Not like this…" Davis cried out in aggravation. "I'm fucking useless and my best friend is going to die because of it." He closed his eyes to hold back his emotions.

Faelan said nothing, knowing Davis was standing on a dangerous precipice. He needed time to regroup and balance himself.

"She didn't deserve that," Davis lamented a few moments later. Opening his eyes, he let out a long, agonized sigh. "She doesn't deserve any of this."

"Brie's tough," Faelan asserted.

"Tough yes, but not unbreakable. If we lose Durov…" He took a deep breath, barely holding back the flood of emotions raging just below the surface.

Faelan had faced his own precipice not that long ago, and felt confident that he could help Davis through it. "You're going to figure it out. There's a way, you just haven't thought of it yet."

"If I could go, then yes, we'd have a chance. But not with me trapped in this useless husk of a body. I can't do a damn thing."

"But you will be able to soon."

Davis shot him an icy glare. "Not soon enough."

Faelan wasn't intimidated by Davis's foul mood because he understood it wasn't personal. It was a normal reaction to recovery; only his was compounded by the threat against the Russian, a man he called brother.

Davis was up against an impossible wall.

"I have a suggestion."

Davis glanced at Faelan dismissively. "Don't you dare give me any platitudes."

Faelan held up his hands. "Hey, I wasn't going there."

Davis sighed. "I apologize. What is your suggestion?"

"If you can't go, then I will go in your stead."

"You are charged with overseeing Lilly. Brie will *not* be put in harm's way again because of my immobility."

"Lilly isn't going anywhere. The baby isn't due to arrive for another month. There's plenty of time, and we have to act fast to save Durov."

Davis frowned. "The sooner the better—if he is to have a chance."

"Then it's settled. I can leave with a day's notice if you need. Just tell me where and who I have to talk to."

"It won't be that simple, and you cannot go alone."

Faelan whistled in exasperation. "You know that's just going to waste time."

"Not finding someone to join you would be a waste of time."

"Why?"

"If you go alone, you are dead."

Brie walked back in with a handful of white towels. She went over to the cup on the ground and dried up the liquid. Afterward, she put the towels in the plastic hamper and walked over to Davis. Before she could speak, he held out his arms to her.

"I'm sorry, babygirl. You didn't deserve to be yelled at for helping me."

Bending down, she melted into his embrace, pressing her cheek against his chest. "It's okay, Sir."

"No, it's not," he replied, petting her long hair. "None of this is okay and I took it out on you."

"I understand. You're afraid—like me..." Her voice broke and she buried her face in his chest.

"I'm terrified," he admitted.

Brie began to cry and Davis did nothing to stop her tears, the two suffering silently together.

When Brie finally quieted, she pulled herself from his embrace and left the room without explanation.

Davis actually smiled when she returned a short time later with a set of fresh towels in her arms. "I can handle a few tears," he admonished.

"That was not a few tears, and I could have kept crying. But it doesn't help you and it doesn't help...him."

Davis nodded, his face straining as he fought again to keep control of his emotions.

While Brie sopped up his wet gown, Davis talked to Faelan about possible candidates. "Gray is out of the question, and Brad's off crutches but his leg is still compromised. I could ask Baron, I'm sure he'd help."

"It's too bad Coen is in Australia," Faelan lamented. "He'd make a good bodyguard."

Davis grunted his agreement.

"What about Ms. Clark?" Brie suggested, gathering the second set of towels and stuffing them in the hamper.

"No way should she be involved," Faelan replied.

Davis mused on her suggestion. "Although they do have a history together…she's still worth considering."

"There's also Captain," Brie added. "I bet his experience would be invaluable."

"Wallace, would you make the calls to our friends? See who is able and willing. Have them meet here tonight."

"Even Ms. Clark?" Faelan asked to confirm. "Isn't she still in Denver?"

"It's only a two-and-a-half-hour flight," Davis replied. "But…she may not be able to leave because of her duties at the Academy."

"Still call her then?"

"I would," Brie piped up.

"And why are you so insistent she be included, babygirl?" Davis asked.

"When things were bad…" Brie paused, as she thought back on it. "Ms. Clark reached out to me. I didn't appreciate just how much she cares about you—and in a time of crisis, it even extended to me."

"She has matured over the years," he replied gruffly, obviously touched to hear of their interaction.

"She loves you, Sir, and she loves Rytsar. I think she should be given the opportunity to help if she can."

"It will be dangerous," he warned, staring directly at Faelan.

"Then you'll need people fully committed," Faelan replied, unruffled.

Davis accepted his allegiance but seemed distressed.

"I don't know how I will repay you for this."

"You already have by finding me a donor," Faelan answered, patting the scar on his abdomen.

"You owe me nothing and you shouldn't go into this based on an obligation of debt."

Faelan smiled easily, shrugging his shoulders. "I'm not. I need to trust my instincts, something Marquis has encouraged me to do, and my instincts are telling me I need to be a part of this."

Brie had remained silent during their exchange, but she wore an odd expression considering the seriousness of the discussion.

It made Faelan curious enough to ask, "What has you all animated?"

She met his gaze, her eyes sparkling with excitement. "I'm sorry, it really has nothing to do with what you two are talking about." She bowed her head and apologized, "Forgive me."

Davis seemed just as perplexed by her sudden elation and commanded, "Go on…explain yourself."

She looked at Davis, grinning. "I'm getting goose-bumps just thinking about it."

"What?"

"I just had a vision about *you*, Todd Wallace," she announced, her finger pointing at him.

"What kind of vision?" Davis asked, clearly interested.

Her smile widened. "The voice of reason."

Faelan frowned. "You're not making sense."

Brie jumped up off her chair, bursting with infectious energy as she explained. "I see you doing a talk show on cable. It's so real that I got the chills."

"This is completely out of left field," he told her, even more confused.

"A talk show, Brie?" Davis questioned, now sounding concerned for her.

Brie's smile only grew bigger. "It's going to happen! I don't know when or how, but it's *going* to happen! I'm seeing a show that debunks the myths about BDSM and…you bring experts in to teach your audience how to practice BDSM safely and effectively. Oh my, people are going to go crazy for it."

Faelan chuckled. "I think you're the one who's crazy."

He looked at Davis. "She's certifiable now."

Brie blurted, "And the best part! It will be called The Voice of Reason."

"Right…"

"Brie, where is this coming from?" Davis asked.

"I know I sound crazy, but I'm telling you it was as clear as day to me. I can *see* it in my mind," she insisted.

Brie looked at Faelan in earnest. "You're so charismatic and knowledgeable. People aren't just hungry to learn about BDSM, they want to know *how* to do it. They're looking for someone they can trust, and you already have a strong following because of the documentary."

Faelan glanced at Davis, shaking his head. "I don't even know why we're discussing this."

Brie punched him in the arm, stating confidently, "It's going to happen."

"I'm glad you feel confident about Wallace's future,

babygirl," Davis said, "But this is neither the time nor the place for such things."

"It's the perfect time," she insisted. Turning to Faelan, she asked, "Do you feel it? A certainty in the core of your being that this is your future? I rarely get a feeling this intense."

He stared at her for several moments. Something *had* stirred his spirit while she was speaking. And even if her vision was completely nuts, he was certain of one thing. He was there to fulfill a purpose—protecting her in whatever capacity necessary.

Brie looked at him with joyous expectation.

Her confidence was disconcerting, but Faelan was acutely aware she was tired, frightened, and running on pure emotion. It was only natural to cling to a dream in the face of an uncertain reality.

She deserved to hold on to something, so he told her, "Whether it plays out the way you envision or not, at least we know I'll be coming back from Russia."

The smile she flashed him was worth indulging her moment of craziness.

Davis looked anxious and unsettled, completely lost in his own thoughts.

Brie stared at her Master in silence, the momentary high already lost as reality set back in. "What can I do, Sir?" she asked, seeking direction.

Davis looked at her with a tender smile. "I can think of only one thing I need right now."

She put his hand up to her cheek and looked deep in to his eyes. "What, Sir?"

"I've heard the recording, but it's no substitute for

the real thing." He moved his hand down and placed it on her stomach. "I really need to hear that heartbeat right now."

Tears came to her eyes and she nodded.

Faelan cleared his throat, wanting to give them space. "I'll go make those calls now."

Brie got up to join Faelan. "I'll walk out with you. I've got a heart monitor to scrounge up."

She turned her head, smiling through fresh tears as she looked back at her husband. "We have to hold on to our hope. Rytsar made us a promise."

Davis gave her a crooked smile as she closed the door.

"Hope…"

Rescue Team

That night Faelan waited in the hospital room, along with Brie and Davis.

"How many do you expect to come?" Brie asked.

"Everyone expressed their desire to help, but such a request requires thoughtful consideration and the ability to leave on a moment's notice. Unfortunately, I can't say."

"Yes, this is *not* a decision to be taken lightly," Davis agreed. "But it's hard, this waiting. Every second wasted could result in his death."

Brie let out an anxious sigh as she stared at the door.

Captain was the first to walk in with Marquis by his side. Neither man had his sub with him, which Faelan found telling.

"I specifically instructed Wallace to leave you out of this," Davis told Marquis.

"It wasn't Mr. Wallace who called me, it was my old friend." Marquis glanced at Captain, who gave a curt nod before walking up to Davis.

"Can I just say that it is a true blessing to see you

awake and recovering."

Davis took his hand in both of his to shake it. "Brie told me how instrumental you were in bringing her to my bedside after the crash. She said she would not have survived the ordeal without you."

Captain gave Brie a sidelong glance. "She exaggerates. Mrs. Davis is strong by her own right."

"Still, you made that difficult time easier for her."

"I did nothing more than you would, Sir Davis."

Baron arrived next. As soon as he saw Davis, his face lit up. Walking straight over, he pulled the man into his arms, not caring about the bed rail between them. "Damn, it's good to see you again."

Davis patted him on the back, smiling when he let go.

"And kitten…how you have grown," he said, looking down at Brie's baby bump. "We'll be hearing the pitter-patter of little feet before we know it."

Brie wrapped her arms around him, closing her eyes and letting herself bask in his comforting presence.

To everyone's surprise, Boa walked in next.

Davis looked to Faelan questioningly, and he shrugged.

"I'm glad to see you, but I have to admit I'm surprised," Davis admitted.

Boa shook his hand, adding a slap on the shoulder. "Mistress and I had a long discussion when we heard from Captain what was going on here tonight. If I can be of any service, I'm willing to offer myself with my Mistress's full support."

Davis looked at him warmly. "I am more moved

than I can express that you have come. However, I do not want to break up partnerships as this will be a dangerous undertaking."

"The offer still stands, Sir Davis."

"Thank you, Boa."

Brie looked up at the beefy sub and smiled. "Yes, thank you. It means the world to us."

He grinned down at her. "We subs have to stick together or how would our Masters survive?"

Brie squeezed his arm as she looked at each person who'd gathered. Faelan could see the hope on her face and he felt the building energy in the room.

There was a chance…

Anderson entered the room, hollering, "Yee-haw!" while twirling his cowboy hat over his head. "Let's go save that Russian bastard."

Davis shook his head. "I'm afraid you're not going."

Anderson frowned. "Why?"

"You are…" Davis started.

"A gimp," Faelan finished.

Anderson flashed Faelan a mocking grin. "I'll show you who's a gimp. Let's wrestle. I dare ya, Wolffie."

"Seriously, Brad," Davis said in a solemn tone. "You're not fully recovered. It is not worth compromising your safety or those of your teammates. I'm sorry, my friend."

Brad glanced over at Faelan. "Don't tell me Wolffie's going."

"He is."

"Damn. It takes just one turtle to ruin an experience of a lifetime."

"Consider yourself fortunate."

"Not going to happen, especially with Wolffie getting to have all the fun. But you know I support you, man. No hard feelings."

Faelan found it amazing that everyone gathered had come knowing that it could mean their own death if they failed, and yet they were here just the same.

Discussions had barely begun when Ms. Clark arrived. Everyone seemed surprised to see her except Brie and Davis.

Ms. Clark paused for a moment in the doorway when she first laid eyes on Davis. "You've returned."

"I have, Samantha."

"I was afraid this day would never come."

"We're fighters."

She nodded, walking into the room in those dangerous stilettos, clicking loudly with each step she took. She looked fierce and in charge until she wrapped her arms around him and openly wept.

The room remained silent as the two longtime friends commiserated together.

Faelan put an arm around Brie while they watched. She looked up at him and whispered, "It's good she's here."

After Ms. Clark dried her tears, she faced the assembly. "So when do we leave?"

"Not so fast, Samantha. This is a covert operation that will only require three people. Any more than that risks exposure."

The men looked at each other.

"How can we choose who goes?"

"The very first question that needs an answer is who here speaks Russian?" Thane asked.

Ms. Clark was the only one to raise her hand.

"By default, you will be going," he announced.

Ms. Clark smiled at Brie with her bright red lips and said in a superior tone, "I always knew learning a second language would pay off."

Brie mouthed the words, "Thank you."

"You should all know I have already requested that Mr. Wallace join the rescue effort," Davis informed them.

The other men looked at each other, now realizing only one remained to be chosen.

All of them asked that they be the one, none backing down. Finally, Davis raised his hand to stop the lively discussion. "I have already eliminated Boa from the list. I do not want Mistress Lou to be without her favorite sub."

Boa sighed, but bowed to the man. "So be it, Sir Davis. I will still assist you in any way I can."

Davis spoke to Marquis next. "As you are aware, I did not want you involved in this. Protect Celestia and the school. That is your service in this operation."

Marquis gave a quick nod. "As Mr. Wallace has been recruited to help in the rescue mission, I will take care of all other matters that require your attention."

Faelan glanced at Marquis, the two exchanging a quick glance that would not be noticed by others but communicated their mutual understanding of the transfer of power.

"So that leaves me and my friend Captain," Baron

stated, puffing up his chest and sporting a beguiling smile aimed at Brie.

She grinned. "You will always be my hero."

"Unfortunately, I will take you up on that offer," Davis stated. "Captain, like Boa, you have a mate and should not be forced to abandon her."

"I disagree," Captain interjected. "Of all those present, I am the one who understands covert operations and military strategies. These Koslov brothers are an organized band of men every bit as dangerous as those I fought against in the war. I am the *only* choice."

"What about Candy?" Davis protested.

"She and I have already talked. I am but one old man. Strategically it makes no sense to sacrifice the strong when the weak are just as capable."

"I can't let you do that," Baron protested.

Captain turned to face him. "Candy has asked that you become her Master if I do not return from this mission."

There was an audible gasp in the room from all attending.

"No!" Davis cried. "Durov would never accept such a sacrifice."

Captain beseeched Baron again. "Would you take my sub as your own if I perish?"

Baron's jaw dropped. "Don't ask this of me."

"Why? Because you do not want her?"

"No, because I don't want to lose you, friend."

Captain put his hand on Baron's shoulder. "There is no one else I would want to care for my pet. She is very precious to me."

Baron looked pained when he answered, "I would be honored to take Candy as my own."

"Good," Captain said, squeezing Baron's shoulder before letting go. He turned to Davis, announcing, "Then it is settled. You have your team. When do we depart?"

Davis said nothing. While everyone watched, he grabbed the rails with both hands and forced himself into an upright position. He looked at all who had gathered. "Thank you for your friendship, your courage, and your selfless hearts. Each one of you here offered the same sacrifice, and for that I will be eternally grateful. Brie and I won't forget this. Rytsar won't forget this." His voice faltered. With tears of gratitude he lay back down in the bed.

Captain took over. "We need nonessentials to leave so that we can formulate our plan and execute it quickly and efficiently."

Baron, Marquis, Anderson, and Boa shook hands with everyone, wishing them good luck and safe travels. Faelan was deeply touched as he shook each of their hands, understanding as they did that this might be the last time they ever saw each other.

Apology

Spending the night talking to Marquis after the meeting, Faelan came to the conclusion there was something he had to do before leaving to face the uncertainty in Russia.

He invited Kylie to lunch, wanting to discuss his idea with her. "I know this may come off odd or a bit forward considering we've really only just met, but I thought I'd run it by you anyway."

"Go ahead, you can ask me anything. I've actually known you most of my life."

Faelan laughed a bit uncomfortably, embarrassed that he didn't remember her even after checking his yearbook to verify she was a student at his school. "Well, had I been paying attention back then I would have known you too, I guess."

"So what is it you're wanting to talk about?"

"I never visited Trevor's grave. I've been terrified of offending Trevor's parents, but maybe closer to the truth, I'm terrified of facing the boy I killed. Spending my whole life running away, I've discovered there are no more places to run."

"Todd, you've spent your entire adult life feeling guilty for breathing."

"No, I'm actually past that now," he insisted.

She looked at him knowingly. "I suspect even now you're thinking of ways to make up for the life you took that day."

He snorted. "Possibly."

"Well, I told you before that our town would welcome you back. They want to make amends for abandoning you and your family like they did. It was a tragic mistake, we all knew that."

Faelan shook his head. "I'll never be able to pay him or his parents back. You can't know how that weighs on me."

Kylie rested her hand gently on his. "You're right. You can't give Trevor his life back, but living in guilt doesn't help him either."

"What about everyone who suffered because of his death, don't you think I owe them something?"

"The only thing you owe them is a life well lived."

Faelan grunted in dissatisfaction. "That's not enough. I have to live the life of two men."

Kylie scooted her chair closer, putting both hands on either side of his face and holding him there as she gazed into his eyes. "Nothing you do will bring him back, but you can respect his memory by living a full and happy life. That's it."

"He was just a kid."

"As were you."

"What about his parents?"

"What about them?"

"Do you think they would be upset when they find out the person who murdered their son had the audacity to visit his grave?"

"I actually think it would give them solace to know that you cared enough to show their son respect, but it doesn't really matter. The Fishers left town shortly after you guys moved away."

"They did?" he asked in shock.

"Yeah, makes what they did to you and your family even more tragic. They spent all that energy running you out, and they didn't even stay."

Faelan sat back in his chair. "I can understand that. Too many memories…"

Kylie kissed him tenderly on the cheek. "I say, give Trevor the honor he deserves so that you can finally let him go."

Faelan felt a stab at his heart, the idea still seeming wrong.

"You can do this."

"If you truly feel that way, I'd like to know if you will join me—tomorrow."

"Tomorrow?" she said with a laugh.

He explained with a white lie, not wanting her to know the details of his upcoming trip to Russia. "I have a lengthy business flight that takes me through the state, and I figured why not get it over with. Why wait any longer?"

Kylie giggled. "Well, I'd call that spontaneous."

He gave her a lopsided grin. "I'm famous for my spontaneity—just ask my friends. Of course, they'd call it something else, but who am I to quibble over words?"

She laughed and announced, "I'm in."

He cocked his head, surprised she was so willing. "Really?"

"Yep, I'd enjoying visiting our old stomping grounds together. And no one is going to believe that Todd Wallace is back."

"Only for a day."

"A day it is then."

"You're serious about doing this?"

"I am if you are."

"Well then, I guess I can give you these now." He handed her two plane tickets.

"Wow, you were totally counting on me saying yes."

"Let's just say it was a risk I was willing to take." He paused for a moment, confessing the truth. "I'll need someone there with me tomorrow."

Kylie smiled. "Then I'm glad you chose me."

Faelan called his parents while they were waiting to board the plane the next morning. "Oh, and by the way I'm bringing someone for you to meet."

"What?" her mother exclaimed on the phone. "Did you work it out with Mary?"

"No, Mom. But Mary and I are still friends."

"I hate how it ended between you."

"But it was for the best," he assured her.

"You know…I was hoping you two would marry

and have kids someday. They would have been so stunning."

Faelan laughed. "I don't know what weed you're smoking, because I don't see Mary *ever* having children."

"Todd!" she protested.

He chuckled but apologized. "Sorry, Mom, but you threw me off with that statement."

"Son," his dad said, taking over the conversation. "Who are you bringing with you?"

"Her name is Kylie, Pop. She went to my high school."

There was dead silence on the other end.

"She's just a friend. We recently connected, but I think you'll like her. Oh, and Mom, she's a few years older than me. Just thought I'd throw that out there."

He heard his father chuckle.

"How much older?" his mother asked, clearly concerned.

"Not much."

Faelan heard a sniffle.

"Mom?"

"I just can't forget how Mary was there for you during your recovery. I saw the difference she made in your life and I truly grew to love that girl."

"There's no reason to stop loving her."

His father was perceptive and asked, "So what's the real reason you're coming, son? I'm not buying this sudden daytrip."

"You know me too well, Pop. It's true, I'm not just coming to see you guys, although it's a perk. I'm also planning to visit Trevor's grave while I'm there."

His mother gasped. "I've been begging you to do that for years."

"I know, Mom, but I wasn't ready until now. You have Kylie to partly thank for that. She's coming with me specifically for that reason."

"Yes," his mother exclaimed. "I've prayed for this ever since the accident."

"It will be good to meet this miracle worker, son."

As they were standing in line to board the plane, Kylie asked Faelan, "You ready to do this?"

Faelan smirked. "No."

She gave him a shoulder bump. "You'll be glad you did, trust me."

He looked down at her smiling eyes and was struck with a thought. *I want to live and breathe you.*

There it was. The moment he knew he was in love with her.

There was no turning back now.

Faelan could feel Kylie trembling as they approached his parents' old mountain cabin. She shifted nervously as she waited for them to answer the door.

"Why so nervous?"

"I'm about to meet Todd Wallace's parents face-to-face at their house. What's not to be nervous about?"

He laughed. "They're just people, Kylie."

Faelan's father opened the door. His gaze landed first on his son, then drifted down to Kylie.

"I think I remember you," he stated.

Her face broke into a huge smile. "You do?"

"Yeah." He nodded. "Didn't you work at the hardware store?"

"I did! Used to work there on weekends and Wednesdays after school."

"Hey, Ada, the girl from the hardware store is here. You remember her, don't ya?" He turned back to Kylie and smiled. "A real nice kid. Real nice."

Faelan felt a bit humiliated that his father remembered her, but felt vindicated when his mother did not. No amount of shared memories on his father's part rang a bell for either of them.

"Well, as you can see, Todd may have gotten the brawn, but not the brains. They all went to his sister," he teased.

Kylie laughed warmly. The sound of her laughter was like refreshing water to Faelan's soul.

Yep, I'm falling hard.

His father had taken an instant liking to Kylie and asked a question he only bestowed on his closest friends. "Hey, you wanna feed the deer?"

"You know it's illegal, Pop," Faelan chastised.

"Your mother and I would rather go to jail taking care of those wild deer than watch them starve because of the severe drought we've had this year."

"But that's nature, Pop."

"Any animal that crosses my property line becomes my responsibility. No government is going to tell me differently."

"I can see it now," Faelan told him, sweeping his

hand in the air. "Elderly Couple Arrested for Illegal Grain Distribution."

"Hey, if that's how it plays out, so be it."

Faelan rolled his eyes, knowing he would never be able to convince either of them to stop.

"I know you disapprove, son, but I'm too old to give a damn."

Kylie laughed. "I like your attitude."

Faelan noticed his mother looking him over, and wasn't surprised to hear her assessment. "You seem a little pale, dear. Is everything okay?"

Faelan glanced at Kylie with a raised eyebrow. "My mother has never stopped treating me like a ten-year-old. Doesn't matter that I'm pushing thirty."

"Oh posh!" his mother complained.

Ada finally turned her attention on Kylie, taking a silent appraisal of her as well. "I think she's worthy," she stated, looking at her husband.

"Worthy of what, Mom?"

"Feeding the critters."

"I love animals!" Kylie said excitedly.

"I could tell that about you. Critters have pure hearts and they can sense that in others. That's why we're picky about who feeds them."

Ada stared at Faelan again and quickly glanced away when he caught her.

"Mom."

She braved a look at her son.

"You don't have to worry about me anymore."

"A mother always worries…"

"Well, I'm doing just fine. That second chance I was

given with the transplant isn't going to be wasted."

He looked at Kylie and reflected on how much had changed recently. He'd been broken inside ever since the accident. No amount of penance had been able to change that but, by some wondrous twist of fate, it seemed this girl made him feel differently—think differently.

Kylie returned his gaze with those expressive eyes that made the world stop for a moment. "I can't wait to see what the future holds for you, Todd."

He felt a chill run through him—not of fear but of expectation.

Kylie was a conduit of positive energy. Ren Nosaka and Marquis Gray had both expressed their high hopes for his future, something Faelan had never felt comfortable with. But when Kylie looked into his eyes, he suddenly felt a sureness he'd never known before.

For the first time in his life, Faelan believed he was ready to accomplish great things.

Turning his attention back to his mother, he told her, "It's time you let go of the immature boy I used to be."

He saw tears form in his mother's eyes.

"No truer words have ever been spoken," his father stated. Standing up, he walked over to Faelan and put his arm around his shoulder.

Faelan looked at him and vowed, "Someday I will make you proud, Pop."

"I already am," he answered without hesitation.

It was Faelan's turn to feel overcome with emotion. He looked at his mother and grinned. "I love you, Mom."

She shook her head, her lips trembling as she turned away.

He felt Kylie tense beside him and realized she saw his mother's reaction as an offense, but he knew it for what it was. This was the first time she no longer saw her little boy when she looked at him, and it overwhelmed her.

"I don't think I ever really told you guys how much I appreciated your support after the accident. I know that it damaged our family's reputation and you lost good friends because of it."

"You're our son. Of course we supported you," his mother exclaimed. "You never meant it to happen. It was simply a terrible accident."

"I was at fault, but you never made me feel like I was a murderer or that you were ashamed of me."

"We weren't, son. Everyone has lost their attention on the road at some point. It is only by the grace of God we all haven't caused an accident."

"Well, I was drowning in guilt. It's the reason I never showed appreciation for all your support—until now."

"Think nothing of it," his father told him.

"We felt your pain, Todd, honey. It was our responsibility as your parents to help you through it, no matter how many times you turned us away."

He chuckled sadly. "I can't tell you how much I resented it back then, Mom. But I am grateful you were so stubborn."

"It's the Wallace way," Ada answered, patting his arm.

"And we wouldn't want it any other way," his father

agreed.

Faelan took a deep breath. "Then this is it. I'm going to visit Trevor's grave after all these years."

His mother took a sharp intake of breath.

"What's wrong, Mom?"

"I've never heard you say his name before."

Faelan nodded. "I know, it's been a long time in coming…"

"Before you go, son…" his father said, getting up and walking over to the liquor cabinet. Taking out a bottle of scotch from the cabinet, he walked back to Faelan and held out the bottle so his son could read the label.

"Pop, we can't drink that."

"Why not? I was given this the day you were born by one of my good friends. I think this is the perfect occasion."

"But weren't you keeping it for something special?"

"It was meant for this day."

Faelan shrugged, shaking his head. "If you insist."

When his father got out four shot glasses, Ada protested. "Don't pour one for me, dear."

"Everyone drinks today, Ada," he insisted, handing her a glass.

He handed the next one to Kylie. "This is a special scotch that has been aged in sherry oak." He gave her a wink, adding, "A rare treat."

Kylie took the glass from him, looking at the amber liquid with interest.

His father handed the next shot to Faelan, stating, "I couldn't be prouder of the man you've become."

With four glasses raised, his father made a toast. "May the years contained in this gift from the gods add vitality and strength to you, my son."

"To my Todd," Ada added.

"And the future," Kylie said.

Knowing what he was about to face, Faelan looked at them with a profound sense of connection. "To the strength of family, friends, and good scotch."

The whiskey was velvety smooth, tasting of orange and nutmeg with a slight hint of fruit. The warmth of the liquor seemed to flow down his throat and straight into his veins. "That's damn good, Pop."

When his father went to pour him another, Faelan stopped him. "Let's save it."

His father furrowed his brow but corked the whiskey, setting it carefully back in the cabinet.

Faelan turned to Kylie. As much as he dreaded what lay ahead, he was ready to face it. "Let's head out before I lose my nerve."

She took his hand and squeezed it. "You've got this."

Faelan approached Trevor's grave with trepidation, a heavy cloud of guilt making it hard to breathe as all those feelings he'd buried long ago came rushing to the surface.

He stared at the gravestone. It should have been his—but it wasn't.

Faelan had lived with that painful truth every day

since the crash.

Kylie stood beside him, a silent pillar of strength as he fought to express his deep sorrow to the boy he'd killed.

"Trevor, I'm sorry."

The crushing weight of those words threatened to undo him.

"Nothing I have done or ever hope to do can make up for the future I stole from you that night. Not only did I end your life, but I changed the lives of everyone who knew you. It's been ten years since your death and I live with that every day… I wish I could change what happened."

Tears pricked his eyes and, for the first time since the accident, he let them fall.

He dropped to his knees, putting his hand on the cold stone. "You deserved a full life, but I took that from you. If you could look into my heart, you would know I'd trade places with you if I could.

"But…I can't. You, your family, and every one of your friends paid the price for my moment of carelessness."

Faelan lay his forehead against the gravestone, the full impact of the pain and grief he'd caused hitting him like a physical blow. He lifted his head and screamed in agony as he embraced the sorrow of Trevor's brutal death and the emptiness that was left.

Kylie knelt beside him, placing her hand on his shoulder in support.

Faelan let the pain release. The unbearable rage and sorrow he'd held in for so long. One moment of carelessness had cost both of them their youth.

When he was emotionally spent, he sat there in silence listening to the birds chirping as a light breeze moved through the trees.

It took some time, but there came a peace.

It was almost disconcerting in its intensity when it hit. Whether it came from Trevor, himself, God, or the Mother Earth he was unsure, but there was a profound power in it.

He looked at Kylie through swollen eyes and smiled.

"Better?"

He nodded, getting up on his feet and holding out his hand to her. "Thank you for this."

She shook her head as she took his hand and lifted herself up. "I didn't do anything."

"Not so. For the first time, I can appreciate that I survived—that I was given a chance to live—and I will not waste another second."

He turned back to the gravestone. "Trevor, I will not be back, but know you will never be forgotten."

Faelan put his arm around Kylie's waist and started walking away. He still carried the heavy weight of all those lives that had been altered because of Trevor's death, but it was balanced by the inner peace he now felt.

Taking in a deep breath, Faelan looked up at the sky and was overcome by a liberating sense of freedom.

It was exhilarating.

Now he could face Russia with nothing to hold him back.

He could finally embrace the future with no regrets—and that made him unstoppable.

Accidental Hero (Ten Years Before)

Visions of how the events would play out made Trevor smile as he drove into town to get the last of his supplies. First, he would take out Chuck, the fucking asshole who'd tormented him since elementary school. Oh, to see the look of shock when the bastard realized he was about to die would be priceless.

Maybe I should snap a pic, he thought.

Trevor could just hear his whimpering voice as he begged for his life… It made Trevor laugh out loud to imagine Chuck's face exploding like a ripe pumpkin.

"Oh yeah…"

Next, he would head to geography class where all the jocks were gathered. Funny that the school had a remedial class designed solely to ensure their star athletes got passing grades no matter how fucking stupid they were.

He would take out as many as he could with his machine gun and if there were any left standing, he would finish them off by throwing a grenade and shutting the door.

Finally, justice would be served after years of being slammed into lockers and mocked relentlessly for being smart.

Then there was Tina… The bitch would pay dearly for humiliating him when he asked her to the dance. The sting of her laughter still rung in his ears to this day. Well, he'd be the one laughing as he picked off each of her cheerleader friends before aiming his gun at her stupid face.

Trevor was forced out of his reverie when car lights blinded his vision. There was no time to react as he watched in terror when the blinding headlights of a car veered into his lane and headed straight toward him.

"You shouldn't have to do this alone."

"I can handle it, June," Cliff insisted.

She put her trembling hand in his arm as he reached for the door handle. "We're both his parents. We should share this burden together."

"I just wanted to protect you, hon."

June stiffened her back and stated, "Together."

He frowned in concern, but opened the door that led down to the basement—Trevor's refuge. The boy had spent countless hours down there in the months leading up to the accident.

Cliff had put this off, focusing all his energies on getting Todd Wallace to leave their town. It pained him too much to be confronted with the sight of his son's murderer walking down the streets while Trevor lay dead in the cemetery.

The time had come to pack up his son's things and attempt to move on from this tragedy. As much as he knew it would hurt, Cliff hoped it would also help the two of them feel closer to their son once it was done.

But as they descended the stairs, despite June's assurances, her tears began to flow. Each step down was a step toward confronting the horrible loss of their only child.

It seemed an impossible task to take that very last step—one no parent should ever have to face.

"Are you sure?" Cliff asked again before they stepped off into the abyss of emotion that waited for them.

June wiped her many tears and nodded.

He flicked on the light.

June gasped.

The sight before them was too shocking to believe.

Cliff was the first to move toward the table laden with military weapons.

"What is this?" June cried as she slowly crept up behind him.

"I have no clue."

A cold chill ran down Cliff's spine. He started sifting through the stockpile of weapons, shocked that his son had been able to amass so many on his own.

"Was he…a gun collector?" June asked naively.

Cliff's gaze landed on the bag of grenades and he shook his head.

June couldn't bear to touch any of the weapons and moved toward a wall plastered with blueprints of Trevor's school. The blueprints themselves were framed in notes he'd handwritten in the margins.

"This doesn't make sense," she insisted, unwilling to get closer to read the words.

Cliff glanced over the blueprints, knowing exactly what it meant. To verify, he read one of the notes printed in Trevor's meticulous handwriting. A numbness crept over him as he recognized the significance of what he was seeing.

"Look at the date."

"What about it?" June asked, refusing to move any closer.

Pointing to it, Cliff found he couldn't stop his hand from shaking. "Trevor was planning an attack on his school the Monday after the crash."

June shook her head. "No… Our son would never—"

"Look around here, June. All of this is his handiwork, all of it."

He picked up a notebook from the table and opened it. "Hell, he even listed the times of execution along with the names of the kids he was planning to kill."

"My son is not a murderer! Trevor would never kill anyone!" she cried.

Cliff flipped through the pages. Something caught his eye, and as he read further he felt the numbness take over his entire body.

"What is it?" June asked when she saw the horrified look on his face.

Cliff snapped the notebook closed, his mouth a hard

line. "It's better you don't know."

"Don't hide anything from me. I'll go crazy if you do."

"June, I'm telling you, there are things best left in the dark."

She tried to grab the notebook from him, yelling, "I have to know!"

Cliff put the book behind his back. "I'll tell you the gist of it, but only if you promise not to read it for yourself."

"Oh my God…what did he write in that notebook?" she whimpered.

Cliff had to force out the words, the numbness finding its way into his heart. "Those kids were not the only ones he planned to kill that day."

She turned white as a sheet. "Who else?"

Cliff shook his head.

"Who else…"

When he remained silent, she stated with fearful resolve, "You promised."

"We were to be his first casualties."

June's chin trembled. She breathed out in a bare whisper, "Why? What did we do to him that he wanted us dead?"

Cliff grabbed her by the shoulders. "Nothing. Not a goddamn thing! The boy was delusional. Wipe it from your mind. Wipe all of it," he commanded with a sweeping motion of his hand.

June looked up at her husband, the devastation of this new revelation adding to the overwhelming loss she was suffering.

"He had some kind of psychotic break," he asserted. "It's the only explanation."

"Cliffie..." June whimpered. "Our lives will be ruined when everyone finds out."

"Nobody knows."

"But when they do—"

Cliff stated in a cold voice, "Nobody knows, and no one ever will."

Faelan never knew he was an accidental hero.

Now the time has come for him, and the entire Submissive Training Center gang, to come together as one.

A sacrifice will have to be made if Rytsar Durov is to survive…

Thank you so much for reading. I hope you enjoyed the 14th book in the Brie's Submission series. The journey continues in **Her Russian Returns**.

Read the next in series.

My dear fans,

I have been working double-time so you will not have to wait long to find out what happens in Russia. ~Red

Preorder **Her Russian Returns** Now!

(Release Date – August 27, 2017)

Over Two Million readers have enjoyed Red's stories.

To find out more visit Red's Website

redphoenix69.com

Follow her on BookBub

bookbub.com/authors/red-phoenix

Facebook: RedPhoenix69

Newsletter: Sign up

redphoenix69.com/newsletter-signup

Twitter: @redphoenix69

Brie's Submission series:

Teach Me #1
Love Me #2
Catch Me #3
Try Me #4
Protect Me #5
Hold Me #6
Surprise Me #7
Trust Me #8
Claim Me #9
Enchant Me #10
A Cowboy's Heart #11
Breathe with Me #12
Her Russian Knight #13
Under His Protection #14
Her Russian Returns #15

Keep up to date with the newest release of Brie by signing up for Red Phoenix's newsletter: redphoenix69.com/newsletter-signup

*Listen to the entire series on Audio

Red Phoenix is the author of:

Blissfully Undone
* Available in eBook and paperback

(Snowy Fun—Two people find themselves snowbound in a cabin where hidden love can flourish, taking one couple on a sensual journey into ménage à trois)

His Scottish Pet: Dom of the Ages
* Available in eBook and paperback

Audio Book: *His Scottish Pet: Dom of the Ages*

(Scottish Dom—A sexy Dom escapes to Scotland in the late 1400s. He encounters a waif who has the potential to free him from his tragic curse)

The Erotic Love Story of Amy and Troy
* Available in eBook and paperback

(Sexual Adventures—True love reigns, but fate continually throws Troy and Amy into the arms of others)

eBooks

Varick: The Reckoning

(Savory Vampire—A dark, sexy vampire story. The hero navigates the dangerous world he has been thrust into with lusty passion and a pure heart)

Keeper of the Wolf Clan (Keeper of Wolves, #1)

(Sexual Secrets—A virginal werewolf must act as the clan's mysterious Keeper)

The Keeper Finds Her Mate (Keeper of Wolves, #2)

(Second Chances—A young she-wolf must choose between old ties or new beginnings)

The Keeper Unites the Alphas (Keeper of Wolves, #3)

(Serious Consequences—The young she-wolf is captured by the rival clan)

Boxed Set: Keeper of Wolves Series (Books 1-3)

(Surprising Secrets—A secret so shocking it will rock Layla's world. The young she-wolf is put in a position of being able to save her werewolf clan or becoming the reason for its destruction)

Socrates Inspires Cherry to Blossom

(Satisfying Surrender—A mature and curvaceous woman becomes fascinated by an online Dom who has much to teach her)

By the Light of the Scottish Moon

(Saving Love—Two lost souls, the Moon, a werewolf and a death wish…)

In 9 Days

(Sweet Romance—A young girl falls in love with the new student, nicknamed "the Freak")

---

9 Days and Counting

(Sacrificial Love—The sequel to In 9 Days delves into the emotional reunion of two longtime lovers)

And Then He Saved Me

(Saving Tenderness—When a young girl tries to kill herself, a man of great character intervenes with a love that heals)

Play With Me at Noon

(Seeking Fulfillment—A desperate wife lives out her fantasies by taking five different men in five days)

Connect with Red on Substance B

Substance B is a platform for independent authors to directly connect with their readers. Please visit Red's Substance B page where you can:

- Sign up for Red's newsletter
- Send a message to Red
- See all platforms where Red's books are sold

Visit Substance B today to learn more about your favorite independent authors.

51615041R00145

Made in the USA
San Bernardino, CA
27 July 2017